LOVE AT FIRST CREPE

HEIDI RENEE MASON

Love at First Crepe © 2017 by Heidi Renee Mason

For information, contact the publisher, Hot Tree Publishing.
WWW.HOTTREEPUBLISHING.COM

EDITING: HOT TREE EDITING
COVER DESIGNER: CLAIRE SMITH
FORMATTING: RMGRAPHX

ISBN-10: 1-925448-89-4
ISBN-13: 978-1-925448-89-4

10 9 8 7 6 5 4 3 2 1

This book is dedicated to my husband, Cameron, who convinced me to journey outside of my comfort zone and write this story. He was the first one to laugh and tell me that I had a winner in the quirky, sassy character of Willow Simpson.

Chapter One

My palms were drenched with sweat. Any second, the moisture was going to start dripping down my fingertips and intermingling with the puddles on the ground. I glanced at the clouds above me and begged the sprinkles to stop falling from the gray sky, at least for a little while. After that, the Pacific Northwest rains could do their worst, and I wouldn't mind. I just wanted the next few moments to be absolutely perfect. I'd waited my whole life for it.

I wiped my hands on my cupcake leggings, trying to appear the calm and poised Portland, Oregon, business owner that I was about to become. I glanced to my left and smiled excitedly at Tate Randall, my lifelong best friend and biggest supporter. He'd put just as much time and effort into getting my food truck, the Dancing Crêpe, ready for the ribbon-cutting ceremony. Without his encouragement, I undoubtedly would not be standing there at that pivotal moment.

I'd wanted to forgo the celebration and just get on with opening my crêpe truck, but the Chamber of Commerce had suggested we hold the ceremony, and Tate had somehow talked me into it. Pomp and circumstance weren't really my cup of tea, but my best friend assured me that the exposure would bring in business. Reluctantly, I'd agreed, since the whole idea of opening a restaurant was to entice customers.

I glanced around, aware that this place, known as Cartlandia, was about to become my home away from home. The crowded lot, a city block long, housed a vast array of trailers touting cuisine from all around the world. It was a foodie's paradise.

I felt a tug on the leash I was holding and glanced down at my cat, Omelet. I'd named her after a breakfast item, and the funny moniker fit the quirky little feline. She was such a good girl, very intelligent, and enjoyed going for walks in the city decked out in her rhinestone collar and matching pink leash. I took her everywhere, except for the dog parks, of course. I often wondered why there weren't any cat parks. It seemed kind of discriminatory. Maybe I should start a petition to open one; Portlanders loved petitions.

To the right of my truck was Seize the Satay, which served Southeast Asian skewers. They were delicious, and I'd frequented the establishment for months. My inability to stay away from those skewers was exactly how I learned that the spot next door, now occupied by my own food truck, was available. Seize the Satay was owned and operated by a kind, middle-aged Indonesian man called Hoang. He said very little, but nodded kindly and smiled every time

I ordered one of his skewers. I noticed that he'd stepped outside to join the ceremony.

To the left of my food truck was Blinis and Blintzes, which offered a variety of the Russian equivalent of crêpes. According to my research, Blinis and Blintzes had occupied its space for several years, and needless to say, the owner probably wasn't thrilled when my crêpe truck rolled up next door.

Granted, it wasn't the best situation to have another crêpe maker parked within arm's reach of your business, but it had been the only space available in Cartlandia. I hadn't yet met the owner, but I noticed that a twentysomething-year-old woman was glaring angrily at me from inside. At least it seemed like she was glaring at me. I was probably just being paranoid as usual.

I averted my gaze from the formidable woman inside Blinis and Blintzes, and tried not to faint as thirty pairs of strange eyes stared at me. *What is a food truck owner supposed to look and act like?* I honestly had no idea. As with most things in my life though, I was quite sure that I fell short. Never able to live up to the expectations of others, I probably wasn't going to be changing anytime soon.

Glancing next to me, I glimpsed the barely concealed frown on my father's face. Speaking of falling short, I'd been doing that for twenty-five years with Barringer Simpson. I was honestly surprised he'd shown up for the ceremony. After all, today was certain to be a major disappointment for the man who'd wanted me to follow along demurely in the Simpson family business.

"Breathe, Willow." Tate leaned over and whispered in my ear. "This is your big day."

"I *am* breathing. If I weren't breathing, I'd be dead," I hissed back at him, frustrated that he knew me so well.

"Just smile. It will all be over before you know it," he encouraged.

For some unknown reason, he was never put off by my difficult personality. He'd more than earned his stripes as my best friend over the years. Tate had made it his life mission to be my personal assistant and protector from the time we were in first grade and Bobby Martin made fun of my red hair and freckles. Ever since that day, he honestly believed that no one could take better care of me than he could. He'd saved my butt more than once over the years.

"…I am pleased to introduce to you, Willow Simpson, the new owner of the Dancing Crêpe!" Somewhere in my brain fog I heard my name being spoken from the front of the crowd.

"You're up, babe." Tate nudged me forward as he took Omelet's leash out of my hand, and I snapped back to reality. "Omelet and I are going to jump inside the food truck and make sure it's ready for business. We'll see you in a minute."

"Don't forget to put Omelet in the carrier behind the boxes. I don't want anyone to see her in there, or I'll be closed down before I even open," I whispered to Tate, and he nodded his understanding.

Again, I wiped my palms on my leggings, took a deep breath, plastered a smile on my face, and stepped to the front of the crowd. I shook the hand of the smiling Chamber of Commerce member who ceremoniously cut the ribbon in front of the Dancing Crêpe. We posed for a photograph, which would probably end up in tomorrow's edition of the local newspaper. I nervously cleared my throat. I'd made it abundantly clear that I wasn't a public speaker and would therefore have no speech to offer. I hoped he hadn't forgotten that very important fact.

Luckily, as soon as the ribbon was cut and the picture was taken, the crowd dispersed and began mingling and talking amongst themselves. *Thank goodness that's over. I survived.* I turned and ran my fingers lovingly across the metal siding of my food truck. She was the realization of a beautiful dream, and if there hadn't been such a crowd, I probably would have kissed her.

I climbed inside the food truck, and Tate grabbed me in a big bear hug. "I'm so proud of you. Your dreams are coming true today!"

"Thanks, Tate. I would have never made it this far if it weren't for you." I flashed him a smile that I hoped conveyed my appreciation.

"Willow, congratulations are in order." Dad's face appeared outside the window of the food truck.

"Thank you, Dad. I appreciate you coming today. I wasn't sure if you would or not," I said quietly.

"You know how I feel about this venture of yours. I think it's ridiculous. A crêpe truck…." He shook his head and his disappointment was more than obvious.

"Yes, I do know how you feel about it, and I've made

my opinion known as well. We are going to have to agree to disagree, because this is reality now," I replied tersely.

"I don't want to argue with you. I came to keep up the appearance of family unity, even if it's not entirely accurate. I knew the press would be here...." His voice trailed off.

"Of course, appearances." I should have known there would be an ulterior motive. There always was.

"I have a meeting. We'll talk soon." Dad cleared his throat and turned to leave.

"Willow, let's take a few photos of you inside of the Dancing Crêpe to post on your Instagram page later. It will be good advertising." Tate touched my arm and guided me gently from the window as my dad walked away.

Even though I was sure he actually wanted to take the pictures, I knew what Tate was really doing. He'd been a buffer between me and my dad for years, and at that moment, I was more grateful than ever for his interference. I really shouldn't expect anything else, but Dad's words cut me deeply. The only reason he'd come today was to keep up appearances, not to support me, his only child.

Dad's reaction wasn't surprising. After all, I had decided not to pursue a career with Simpson Coffee. I had nothing personal against caffeine; in fact, I'd always been a huge fan. I was only interested in drinking it though, not selling it. So, rebelling as usual, I insisted upon following the entrepreneurial idea of owning my own restaurant.

For as long as I could remember, I'd spent my days in the kitchen with the estate's cooks, learning the tricks of the trade. I could make a fluffy soufflé at the age of nine, a feat that often took cooks years to perfect. While other girls my age were hanging out at the country club, I was elbow-deep in bread dough, always honing my craft.

Cooking was my passion, and the kitchen was the only place I'd really ever felt at home. Honestly, Dad wasn't all that interested in his parental role, and he was often at a loss as to what to do with me. He loved me in his own way, I supposed, but affection wasn't his strong suit. He had no idea how to show his love in any way except to throw money at me. Sadly, money was the one thing I'd never wanted.

"Go outside and take some selfies in front of the sign, Willow. I've got things under control here when the crowd shows up," Tate said, in an attempt to distract me from Dad's uncomfortable "congratulations" and abrupt departure.

I walked to the side of the food truck and took a look around. As of that moment, I would be spending a large chunk of my life in Cartlandia, and I hadn't really become personally acquainted with the neighboring business owners. Other than meeting Hoang when I had my mouth stuffed full of beef skewers, I knew little else about the surrounding food community. I was sure we would all end up being great friends though, considering we would have a lot in common.

I heard a loud voice from next door at Blinis and Blintzes. Turning in that direction, I was surprised to discover that the angry-sounding comment was directed at me. Of course, it was spoken in what I assumed was Russian, so I had no idea what the exotic-looking young woman was saying. She was about my age and would have been quite beautiful had it not been for the murderous rage contorting her face.

"Willow…." Tate's voice had taken on a cautionary tone. He was already in protective mode, but I shook my head at him, silently warning him to let me handle the situation.

"I'm sorry, miss, but I didn't really understand what you said to me. My name is Willow Simpson. I'm the owner of the Dancing Crêpe." I smiled kindly and extended my hand to the woman standing in front of me.

"I said you are not welcome here," she replied in her thick accent, refusing to shake my hand.

"What's your name?" I had intended to remain civil, but her greeting let me know that I was going to need to pursue another course of action.

"My name is Katya. This is my food truck." She gestured toward Blinis and Blintzes. "I was here first, and you need to go."

"Well, Katya, I'm not sure how I'm supposed to respond to that, but unfortunately, it doesn't appear that your opinion matters very much, seeing as I'm here to stay." The smile remained on my face, but my words were as cold as ice.

"We will see about that," Katya replied through gritted teeth. "And did I see a cat in your food truck? I wonder if the health inspector knows about that."

"It seems to me that you have your own business to worry about, so you should probably stay out of mine," I challenged. "But just keep in mind that I'm not going anywhere and neither is my cat. She's not a fan of mean people, so you might want to steer clear of her."

Katya turned swiftly and went back inside her food truck,

spewing a string of what were probably Russian profanities in the process. I was sure I was better off not knowing what she said. I shook my head in disbelief. *The nerve of that woman!*

"You good?" Tate questioned as I went back inside. Omelet meowed at me from her crate in the corner.

"I'm just fine. How dare she try to ruin this day for me? And while I'm at it, how dare my dad be anything but happy for me? What's wrong with people, anyhow?" I stormed.

"Well, you know I'm happy for you, babe. This is your big day. Don't let anyone mess it up. You've been dreaming of this your whole life."

"That's why you're my best friend. I can always count on you." I kissed Tate on the cheek and felt him stiffen. *That's strange.* I'd kissed him on the cheek a thousand times and he'd never reacted that way before.

"No time for mushy business. The line is starting. Time to show 'em what you've got, Willow." Tate recovered from the awkward moment quickly, but I knew something was up. I'd get to the bottom of it eventually, but I didn't have time right then. The crowd was arriving, and it was go time.

Chapter Two

The next two weeks passed by in a blur. I spent nearly twelve hours every day at the Dancing Crêpe, and I loved every minute of it. It was everything I'd ever dreamed of and more. After working fourteen days straight, without a break, I'd been persuaded by Dad to meet him and Elizabeth, my stepmother, for lunch.

I still hadn't figured out what my normal operating hours would be, and had so far been practically living in my food truck. Since it was a relatively slow day, and since I was always trying to get on Dad's good side, I reluctantly closed for the day and agreed. Besides, I really did need a day off. I begged Tate to come with me for moral support.

Elizabeth was third in the long line of stepmothers I'd had the displeasure of knowing since my mother's death when I was just five years old. Elizabeth was only twenty-seven, just two years my senior, and she was by far the most horrible one yet. She was everything I aspired not to be. She and Dad had been married only a year, but in my opinion, it was the worst year ever.

My father was blind to his new wife's ambitions, but I knew a schemer when I saw one, and Elizabeth was the queen of gold diggers. I'd tried to convince my father not to marry her. *A lot of good that did.* If anything, my intense dislike for Elizabeth seemed to make the woman even more appealing to him. Never one to consider my feelings, good old Dad married her anyway.

Elizabeth was a smooth operator, for sure. She had her French-manicured nails sunk deep inside Dad, and there was nothing I could do about it except stand by and watch the soap opera unfold. It was like standing on a train track while an express raced straight toward me. I knew the crash was coming; it was just a matter of time before the impact.

The disgruntled string of wives trailing behind my father was the main reason I wholeheartedly believed that the notion of love was nothing but a lie. From what I'd learned in life, love didn't make the world go round. Money did.

Earlier that morning, I found out that Elizabeth's best friend, Cinnamon St. James, would be joining us for lunch as well. Elizabeth was bad enough on her own, but when you added Cinnamon into the mixture, it was more than I could stomach. The two of them made me want to vomit.

Knowing I would need some caffeine to fortify me, Omelet and I headed into the Simpson Coffee shop right around the corner from my apartment. Everyone in there knew us, and stopping by was a part of our daily routine.

"Morning, Willow. Hey, Omelet," the green-haired barista called as we walked through the door. "The usual?"

"Yep, thanks, Suzanne." I smiled at her, and Omelet and I took a seat at the table in the corner.

"The usual" for me was a butterscotch latte with extra butterscotch. Omelet had her own special drink, and all the baristas knew exactly what she wanted. They'd coined it the "feline frother," which was really just steamed soy milk, since Omelet was lactose intolerant. It was served in a shallow mug for easy lapping. There weren't any other cats that frequented the coffee shop, but I'd learned pretty quickly that Omelet wasn't at all like other cats. Since Portland was an obsessively pet-friendly city, my little furball went almost everywhere with me, including work. As long as it didn't get back to the health inspector, we would be fine, although I probably shouldn't risk it. If I didn't want to put my livelihood in jeopardy, I should start leaving her at home. I would have to talk with Omelet about the situation. She would understand. I hadn't really checked the regulations, but I had a feeling that Omelet's presence in my food truck might not be appreciated.

Glancing out the window, I sipped my latte and Omelet lapped her frother as we watched the throngs of people pass by. The city was a hubbub of activity, but that was nothing new. Weekends were always busy, and I knew I would probably regret closing the Dancing Crêpe for the day. I'd better get some good daughter points in with Dad for doing it.

I heard the bell on the front door jingle and felt my face flush as the man walked inside. Even Omelet looked up from her drink and stared at him as he entered the coffee shop. I had no idea who he was, but I'd seen him around a lot. I had a feeling he lived somewhere in my apartment building, but other than that, and the fact that he was devastatingly handsome, I had no other information.

He placed his order and stepped to the other end of the counter, which was right next to my table. I tried to avert my gaze, but I wasn't fast enough. He caught me looking in his direction and smiled. I shivered a little, in spite of the fact that it was warm in the room, and returned his smile. He made my insides feel like jelly, and I wasn't sure if I liked the feeling or not.

"How's your drink, Willow?" Suzanne called from behind the counter.

Tearing my eyes away from the handsome stranger, I replied, "Wonderful as usual, Suzanne." I was just about to take another sip when I heard his voice.

"Willow… that's a pretty name," he said.

"Thank you. My mother was a hippie," I blurted.

"That's… nice." He chuckled.

"Yeah, well, you probably figured that with a name like Willow." I cringed as I heard myself talking, but was unable to stop. "I'll bet you have a nice, sensible name like Tom."

"Actually, my name is Marcus Tucker." He laughed.

"Hmm, you look like a Marcus. Sexy name for a sexy man." I clamped the hand that wasn't holding the coffee over my mouth. I couldn't believe I'd just said that out loud.

"It's a pleasure meeting you, Willow," he replied with a grin.

"You too." I took the final sip of my latte and was relieved to see that Omelet had finished her drink as well. "I'm going to take off now and go pull my foot out of my mouth. See you around."

I grabbed Omelet's leash, waved awkwardly at Marcus, and attempted a quick exit. Unfortunately, Omelet and I couldn't stop staring at our new acquaintance, and we both ran smack-dab into the glass door. My cat seemed just as smitten with him as I was. We obviously had the same taste in men.

Peeling myself off the glass, I rubbed my forehead. I could only hope that Marcus hadn't seen me run into the door, but my hopes were immediately dashed when he jogged across the room and placed his hand on my arm.

"Are you all right? It looked like that hurt," he asked.

"Nothing wounded but my pride. I'll see you around," I answered quickly.

My face was on fire, and I wanted to die of embarrassment. *Way to go, Willow. You just called a complete stranger sexy, and then ran into the door because you couldn't stop staring at him!* I felt his eyes follow me as I practically ran from the coffee shop. I wanted nothing more than to crawl under a rock and die, and I vowed to make it a point never to see him again. Avoiding that man at all costs was my new mission in life. He probably thought I was an idiot, and he would be correct. *I should not be trusted around normal people.* My phone beeped and I opened the incoming text from Tate.

Tate: I'll meet you in front of Bonjour in twenty minutes. You owe me. You know how I feel about Elizabeth and Cinnamon.

Willow: Yeah, I owe you. But you know I would kill them both without you there to stop me. I'm running Om elet home and I'll be right there.

I dropped my cell phone into my purse and walked around the block to drop Omelet off at home. After getting her settled and locking up my apartment, I hopped on the MAX and took it across town. I stood by the window, holding on tightly to the bar since I was a klutz and would more than likely fall down from the motion of the bus. Glancing out the window, I noticed the throng of protesters blocking the street up ahead. Hopefully they would move soon, or else I was going to be late meeting Tate, and I despised being late.

As I watched the large crowd, I wondered what cause was being protested. The hipsters of Portland tended to be quite active in making their voices heard. From the signs they were waving, I gathered that several people were unhappy about the idea of Daylight Savings Time. I couldn't say I blamed them. Had I known the march was happening sooner, I might have even joined them. There was nothing worse than having five o'clock in the morning arrive an hour earlier each spring.

The crowd parted and made way for the MAX, and we continued on our way. Jumping out at the stop next to Bonjour, I saw that Tate was already there, leaning casually against the brick building. My best friend was a dashingly handsome blond-haired, green-eyed firefighter, and I couldn't help but notice the glances of admiration he received from a group of women passing by. Tate, however, was completely oblivious to the charms that were so obvious to everyone else. He always had been.

"Thanks for meeting me. You know I can't handle those two alone." I hugged him, grateful once again that he was always there for me.

"You're welcome, but if Cinnamon starts flirting with me as usual, you're going to need to tell her to stop. I don't want to be rude, but she's always putting her hands on me." Tate wrinkled up his nose.

"Don't worry. It always gives me great pleasure to put her in her place." I laughed.

I was about to elaborate on all the things I'd like to do to Cinnamon when I heard the clickety-clack of high heels on the sidewalk. I didn't even need to turn around to know that it was Elizabeth and Cinnamon.

They walked side by side, perfectly in step, as if strolling down the sidewalk was a choreographed routine. They were even dressed alike in black skinny jeans, and tight, hot-pink shirts with plunging V-necks. More often than not, they coordinated their outfits, and they had for as long as I could remember. I kept thinking that they would grow out of it, but they never had. Their perfect blonde hair was as smooth as spun glass, and nothing about them was out of place. It was disgusting.

The four of us had an interesting history. We'd grown up in the same community, and we'd attended the same prestigious schools. Elizabeth and Cinnamon were two years older than Tate and me, but our families had all run in the same high-class circles for as long as I could remember. The Barbie twins had made my life miserable as a kid, and they continued to do so. It was a million times worse now that Elizabeth was my stepmother. When Barringer Simpson married a woman who was basically the same age as his daughter, some people were shocked. I wasn't one of those people. His taste in wives—other than my mother—had always been questionable.

On top of the feelings of mutual dislike between me and the two women, Cinnamon had been after Tate since we were kids. She'd always had a thing for him and was constantly trying to get his attention. Despite her best efforts, he'd made it perfectly clear that he was my friend. That hadn't won me any points with her, and probably made the two of them hate me even more.

As much as I disliked them, I couldn't help being jealous of both Cinnamon and Elizabeth. They were the spitting images of what my father wanted me to be, and the opposite of the person I really was.

"Willow, Tate, thank you for meeting us," Elizabeth said haughtily, looking down her nose at me. She was at least a head taller than I was, and was made even more so by her incredibly high heels.

"Where's my father?" I felt a sinking feeling in the pit of my stomach.

"Barringer couldn't make it. Something suddenly came up, a business meeting or whatever. He suggested that we meet without him." Elizabeth flipped her hair as she explained the situation.

"Of course he did. I should have known better than to close up the food truck for him," I huffed. "If it's all the same to you, we can just skip it. I'm sure you don't want to have lunch with me any more than I want to have lunch with you." I rolled my eyes.

"I promised your father we would, and so we will. And if we don't, he'll know it was your fault." She smirked.

"Everything is always my fault. He's used to that. Fine, whatever, let's get this over with." I stomped ahead of them and into the building.

That superior behavior was so typical of her. She would like nothing more than to make me look bad in my father's eyes, not that she had to work very hard at it. I managed to do just fine on my own in that area. It was exasperating that Dad was always trying to come up with ways to throw Elizabeth and me together. If he thought we were going to get along with each other, he had another think coming.

I chose a booth in the corner, away from the rest of the crowd in the bistro. At least the food there was good, if not the company. Tate slid in next to me, and our unfortunate lunch companions scooted in across from us. I had no idea what we were going to talk about. We didn't even like each other, except for Cinnamon, who liked Tate a little too much.

"I'm glad you're here, Tate. Cinnamon and I have been meaning to get in touch with you about something," Elizabeth began.

"In touch with me? About what?" he questioned,

obviously confused.

"Some of the ladies at the country club have wanted to do a fundraiser, and we've been looking for a worthy cause. We're thinking that the fire station might benefit from a sizable donation, and we were hoping to organize a Fireman's Ball, with all of the proceeds going to the station." My stepmother admired her French manicure as she spoke.

"Yeah, sure, that's very generous. There are always things we can use money for. What made you think of the fire station?" Tate asked.

"It was actually Cinnamon's idea. She's the head of the committee," Elizabeth stated.

"Yeah, you know, firefighters are so brave, and I just thought there was no better place to donate our money." Cinnamon grinned widely, baring her perfect teeth and looking as if she'd like to eat Tate whole. He squirmed uncomfortably beside me. I knew this charity bit was just her way of trying to get on Tate's good side.

"It's a good idea, Cinnamon. Thank you," he replied kindly.

Even though he disliked her immensely, he had a hard time being rude to anyone. I, on the other hand, did not have that problem. "I'm guessing the fact that you've always been hung up on Tate had no bearing whatsoever on your choice for a donation recipient, right, Cinnamon?" I chuckled.

"I'm guessing that good fashion sense had no bearing whatsoever on your choice in wardrobe today, did it, Willow?" she retorted.

"If by good fashion sense you're referring to the fact

that I'm a unique individual, rather than simply mimicking my best friend, you can say whatever you would like about me," I returned.

"You've always been jealous of me. When are you going to admit it?" Cinnamon sneered.

"When you admit what a horrific witch you are," I replied.

"Ladies, you're drawing a crowd, and not in a good way," Tate said quietly.

I took a deep breath, trying to get my childishness in check. It seemed that no matter how old I was, when the two of them were around, I reverted to snide teenager mode. I couldn't help myself. It was a reflex. The only way to solve the problem was to remove myself from the situation.

"You know what? Let's not do this. You can tell my father whatever you like, Elizabeth, but I'm going home now." I nudged Tate, who scooted out of the booth, and I followed him.

"You're such a child, Willow. You just can't be civil, can you? Don't worry, I'll tell Barringer exactly what happened." Elizabeth's piercing blue eyes bored through me.

"I have no doubt that you will, and I'm sure that I'll be the one to blame and you'll be completely faultless." I turned away from her.

Elizabeth continued talking, however, ignoring the fact that I was done. "Tate, I'm going to need your chief's phone number to get in contact with him about the fundraiser."

"I can't give you his personal number without his permission," Tate answered. "I'll write down the station phone number though."

"Fine then. I'll write down my number and you can pass it along to him and let him know I'll be calling." She pulled out a notebook, ripped off a piece of paper, and scrawled something onto it. Tate quickly stuffed it into the pocket of his jacket.

"Let's go, Tate," I demanded, stomping out the front door. He followed closely behind me.

"I'm happy to leave, Willow, but I was looking forward to lunch. I'm hungry," he complained as we walked out the door of the restaurant.

"You're always hungry. Come back to my place and I'll make us something. I'm sorry, but I couldn't stand to breathe the same air as those two for another second." I rolled my eyes.

"Fine by me. Your food is way better than the food at Bonjour anyway," Tate answered.

"Yeah, it is," I agreed. "Let's go."

I grabbed his hand, just as I'd done a million times before. Instead of holding on though, he stopped walking, looked at me strangely, and dropped my hand.

"What was that for?" I asked, completely confused.

"What?" he replied, shoving his hands into the pockets of his jeans.

"What's up with dropping my hand? Did I do something wrong?" I questioned.

"No, sorry, don't worry about it. It's all good. Let's go make lunch." He continued walking toward the MAX with his hands still stuffed in his pockets. We rode the bus to my apartment in silence.

He'd tried to pretend that his reaction wasn't unusual, but I knew better. Something was off with him lately, but I couldn't quite put my finger on it. Tate and I had always been physically affectionate with each other, but lately it seemed that any time I touched him, he recoiled. *What does that mean?* Then all at once, it hit me. I knew exactly what was wrong. *Tate's interested in someone and he hasn't told me about her! Tate has a girlfriend!* That had to be it.

Tate and I had always told each other everything, so why hadn't he told me about this girl? We'd both dated people casually over the years, but neither of us had ever had a serious relationship. I was a complete mental case when it came to love, but sometimes I wondered why Tate hadn't found someone. I mean, he was a complete catch! He was gorgeous, responsible, trustworthy, stable, and everything a girl could ever want. Yes, it was very strange that he hadn't yet settled down with a nice girl.

My emotions were conflicted as I thought about Tate and his mystery woman. *Is she pretty? Is she sweet? Why don't I know about her?* It was the only time I could remember my best friend keeping a secret from me. Well, now that I knew, I was going to have to figure out a delicate way of getting him to confide in me. Of course, I had to meet her immediately. He couldn't date anyone without my approval.

I tried to picture Tate in a serious relationship with a woman, and I began to feel strange. It felt like my insides were gnawing at themselves. I was probably just hungry, right?

Twenty minutes later, we were in my kitchen and I was gathering the ingredients to make bacon-wrapped scallops. It was one of my favorite meals, and after having to deal with Cinnamon and Elizabeth, I deserved it. Before long, the savory aroma in my kitchen had my mouth watering in anticipation. We made quick work of the delicious lunch, and then decided to watch a movie together.

Tate had been quiet and distracted since we'd arrived back at my place, and I was even more determined to get him to tell me about the mystery girl. Once we had flopped onto my couch, I dove right in.

"Is something bothering you today? You're kind of quiet," I began.

"No, I'm fine." He smiled, but I saw right through him.

"You think I don't know you better than that? Spill it," I demanded.

"I can't." Tate turned his face away from mine.

"What do you mean, you can't? You've told me everything since we were six years old," I argued.

"Well I can't tell you this," he said stubbornly.

"Tate, there's nothing in the world you can't tell me. I'm your best friend." I was starting to get a bit irritated. The secrecy was very much unlike him.

"Can you just drop it?" He stood up from the couch and turned his back toward me.

"No, I will not drop it. What's going on, Tate?" I rose and positioned my body in front of his, forcing him to focus his green eyes on me.

"Do you really want to know? You don't know what

you're asking," he warned.

"Of course I want to know!" He seemed to be having a hard time saying the words. *Maybe I should make this easier on him. Maybe I should tell him that I already know.* I placed my hand on his arm. "It's okay, Tate. I already know what you're going to say. Who is she and where did you meet her?" I smiled, congratulating myself for being so intuitive.

"What are you talking about?" He looked completely confused.

"The girl you're involved with. Who is she?" I laughed at his shocked look. He was probably surprised that I'd figured it all out on my own.

"You think I'm involved with someone? That's what you think this is about?" Tate spoke slowly.

"Yeah, I figured it out on the bus. It all makes sense. I've noticed that you seem to be dodging me when I try and grab your hand, and when I kissed your cheek the other day, you pulled away. At first, I was confused, but now that I know you have a girlfriend, it all makes sense. You wouldn't want her getting the wrong idea about us. She's probably going to have a hard time with how close we are though. Don't you think? Will I like her?" I realized I was talking at a mile a minute and rambling on without really letting him answer any of my questions, so I paused.

"You've got it all wrong, Willow. You are so far off course right now…." Tate looked a bit sick, and I couldn't believe he was having such a hard time telling me about his new girlfriend.

"It's all right. I was a little surprised when I first figured it out, and I am still a little irritated that you didn't tell me sooner, but I forgive you. Now, tell me who she is." I smiled encouragingly at him.

"Are you really that blind? Willow, it's you," Tate answered quietly.

"Good one. You're funny." I laughed, punching him in the arm playfully. He always knew how to make me smile.

"Please don't laugh at me. I'm in love with you. I think I always have been, but lately… it's become… clearer to me." The look on his face was deadly serious, and it immediately wiped the smile off mine.

"In love? With me? Are you sure?" *I'm going to throw up.*

"I'm more sure of this than I've ever been of anything."

"Wow… I think I need to sit down." I tore my gaze away from his, but not before I saw the look of raw sadness there. Obviously that wasn't the answer he was hoping for, but it was the best I could manage under the circumstances.

I walked toward my couch on legs that felt like Jell-O, and collapsed into the soft cushions. Tate followed and sat down beside me. My head was spinning, and I couldn't bring myself to look at him. *In love with me? We're best friends. A person doesn't fall in love with his best friend. Does he?*

Tate bounced his legs up and down nervously. I knew he was waiting for my response. I had no idea how much time had passed, but it seemed like at least twenty years. *Say something, Willow.* Clearing my throat, I tried to find the proper words.

"Tate, we've been through so much together. Maybe it's not romantic love you're feeling. Maybe it's the best friend kind of love," I suggested gently.

"Babe, I know exactly what I feel for you, and there's nothing even remotely friendly about it. I've tried my best to hide it, but I just can't anymore. Every time we're together, I want…."

"You want what?" I turned my face toward his and looked into his beautiful emerald eyes. There was such a depth of emotion in them that I wanted to look away. Before I could move though, Tate reached out, caressed my cheek with his fingertip, and said, "I love you, Willow."

I should have moved away, I supposed, but I didn't. Instead, my face inched closer to his and our lips touched. In all the years we'd been friends, I had never even thought about kissing Tate, but at that moment, I wondered why. Rather than being awkward, it felt fantastic! I wanted more.

Scooting closer to him on the cushion, I wrapped both arms around his neck. He moaned something, but for the life of me, I had no idea what it was. I didn't have a clue what had come over me, but I pushed him back on the cushion and angled my body so that I was on top of him. He tasted so good, like peppermint and lemons.

Tate tangled his hands into my hair and pulled me closer. The room was spinning; time was speeding by and standing still all at the same time. It seemed that neither of us wanted to come up for air. We probably would have kept going for days if my leg hadn't cramped up at that moment. But it did, and as I slid back into reality, a nagging voice screamed wildly inside my head, *you're kissing Tate!*

"Whoa, okay… time-out," I muttered as I pulled myself into a sitting position. I fixed my clothes and smoothed my hair.

"A time-out is not necessary. I think we were doing just fine." He smiled lazily.

"That was… wonderful… and… completely unexpected," I managed.

"But pretty great, nevertheless," he added.

"That's beside the point." I stood up and began to pace back and forth across my living room. "That can never, *ever* happen again."

"What do you mean? Give me one good reason why it can't happen again." Tate rose and stood in front of me, forcing me to stop pacing and look at him.

"Because you're my very best friend in the entire world, Tate, that's why." My voice rose.

"And you're mine, but it doesn't change the fact that I'm in love with you." He put his finger under my chin and tilted my face up toward his.

I felt the magnetic force and wanted nothing more than to just obey, but I couldn't do that. "Tate, here's the deal. You know I'm a mess. I'm a disaster. I don't do relationships. I don't even know a single person who has a healthy relationship. How could I even hope to think I could do it? Anyone who gets involved with me is doomed. Don't you remember John? We only went on three dates and he told me I was so crazy that he would never date again! I won't do that to you. I won't," I argued.

"You're wrong, Willow. You and me, we can make it work. I know we can. I love you," he insisted.

"Tate, I love you too, but I don't know if it's the same kind of love. You're my anchor. I depend on you for everything, and maybe it's selfish of me, but I don't want to lose that. I *can't* lose that. And I just know that's what would happen if we got together in that way. So I can't. And I don't want to hurt you, or make you angry. Please, don't be angry," I begged, grasping his hands desperately with mine.

"I could never be angry with you." He squeezed my hands.

"Okay, then. Can we just… I don't know… put this on the back burner for a while? Let me think about what you've said to me. Can I have some time to process it all?" My brain was spinning a thousand miles an hour.

"Yes, I'm sorry. I didn't even give you time to prepare for it. I just… couldn't keep it in anymore." He shrugged.

"I'm glad you told me, really. I'm shocked, and I honestly thought your big secret was that you'd met some fantastic girl. For your sake, I'm desperately sorry that I'm the girl. You really got the raw end of the deal by falling for me." *Poor Tate, he deserves so much better.*

"You're always selling yourself short. There couldn't possibly be a better woman for me than you," he replied.

"I don't know… are things going to be weird between us now?" I couldn't handle a rift in our relationship. I needed him too much.

"No more weird than it usually is." He laughed good-naturedly, but I couldn't help but notice how sad he looked.

"Should we start the movie?" I suggested, not really sure what else to say.

"If it's okay with you, I think I'm going to head out. I need a little time to clear my mind." He squeezed my hands one last time before letting go.

"Sure, that's fine," I replied, swallowing hard over the lump that had lodged in my throat.

"We'll talk soon," he said as he turned away and headed quickly out the front door.

The sound of the door closing behind him seemed inordinately loud in the empty room. My hands began to shake, and my eyes blurred with unshed tears. I knew I'd hurt him deeply, but I had no idea what else I could have done. The very idea of Tate and me falling in love was ridiculous, wasn't it? There was no way we could make a relationship work, and soon, he would come to his senses and realize that too. Then we could go back to the way things had always been.

I'd done the right thing; I was sure of it. I collapsed into the nearby chair and looked around my apartment. I was alone, and that was just the way I liked it. Being unattached was the best thing for a girl like me. I was damaged goods, and I had way too much baggage for any chance at a normal relationship. *But if I've done the right thing, why do I feel so empty? Why does it feel so wrong?*

Glancing beside me at the arm of the chair, I saw Tate's jacket. I laid my head on it and breathed in the scent of him. I needed him in my life, and I couldn't do anything that might jeopardize that. He'd said he needed some time to clear his head, so I would give him that. Tomorrow, I would call and tell him he'd forgotten his jacket. By then, he should be over this nonsense of thinking he was in love with me, right?

Chapter Three

I plodded through the rain, trying my best to avoid the vast array of puddles decorating the gray streets in front of me. Omelet trotted beside me, dressed in her purple rain jacket. She hated having wet fur, so she actually loved wearing it. Her adorableness was off the charts.

Gathering my own raincoat close to my body, I adjusted the hood. Like most Portlanders, I didn't use an umbrella; I believed they were completely unnecessary. Only tourists used them, and locals could spot an outsider from a mile away.

Some people grew tired of the seemingly constant drizzle that was characteristic of the Pacific Northwest's climate, but I wasn't one of them. Rainwater coursed through my veins. Having lived there my entire life, it was part of me.

Sloshing through the puddles, Omelet and I arrived

at Cartlandia and I fished in my purse for the keys to the Dancing Crêpe. I unlocked the door, and we slipped inside, out of the rain. Shaking the water off my coat, I turned on the small space heater before flipping on the lights inside my restaurant on wheels. I removed Omelet's raincoat, and she trotted over to her cat crate in the corner. She yawned, stretched, and closed her eyes. It was time for her nap.

Arriving at work always gave me the feeling of coming home. I was only a few weeks into owning the Dancing Crêpe, but I still felt like pinching myself to be sure I wasn't dreaming. My little restaurant gave me such a thrill. Customers asked nearly every day how I'd come up with such an unusual name for the food truck, and I enjoyed telling the story. The Dancing Crêpe was named in honor of my love affair with ballet.

Growing up, Dad insisted that a girl of my social standing should be well-versed in the arts. So as a child, I was chauffeured to piano lessons, voice lessons, and art lessons. Much to Dad's dismay, I was an abysmal failure at all of them.

I also took ballet lessons from the time I was five. Admittedly, I was too clumsy to be any good, and I could write a book about all the dance-related injuries I'd sustained due to my lack of grace. Once, I'd ended up with two broken legs when I'd fallen out of a turn en pointe. I'd rolled around school in my wheelchair for weeks being tormented by my classmates for being such a klutz. I was publicly humiliated on many occasions by Ms. Solange, my stern-faced ballet instructor, whose slicked-back bun pinched her severe face tightly. "Willow Simpson, your arms look like wet noodles! Fix them!" Her words had cracked like a whip.

In spite of my awkwardness, I developed a love for dance, and I still took a barre class every week to stay in shape. I once dreamed of dancing professionally, but it didn't take long for me to realize I had neither the skill nor the discipline to bring that ambition to fruition.

I'd long since recovered from the disappointment of not becoming a prima ballerina, but I remained passionate about ballet. The crêpes on my food truck menu were named after ballet terms, such as the grand jeté and the piqué. Since I wasn't cut out for the professional dance world, it was my clever way of bringing dance into my daily life.

So far, I was doing well. If business kept booming, within five years I would be financially stable enough to open a brick-and-mortar restaurant. I knew my dream was within reach, and I wouldn't let anything or anyone get in my way. Cooking was my life, and I didn't need any distractions.

Mixing up the batter for the day's crêpes, I composed a mental checklist of all I needed to accomplish. I had a feeling it was going to be a very busy day, and that made me happy. Unfortunately, I remembered I'd also agreed to have dinner that evening with Dad and Elizabeth. At that moment, I was kicking myself for agreeing to go, but at least I'd managed to convince Tate to go with me. I knew I could handle it if he were there.

In the days since he'd confessed his feelings for me, our time together had been a bit strained. It was like the elephant in the room that no one wanted to talk about. Actually, I was the one who didn't want to talk about it. I was sure he would have been more than willing to talk at length about the way he felt. The problem was the way I felt, and the main issue was that I had no idea.

So, since I couldn't jeopardize losing Tate, my solution was to simply pretend that the whole "I'm in love with you" discussion had never happened. If I ignored it long enough, it would all go away. Or so I hoped. It was working for me—for the most part—but I didn't think Tate was enjoying it at all.

My phone beeped, and I opened the text from Tate. *It's so weird how he always texts or calls me at the exact moment I'm thinking about him.*

Tate: I hate to do this to you, but I can't go to dinner with you tonight. I just got called in to work. I'm really sorry.

Willow: Ugh. I can't do it alone. It's okay. I'll just cancel.

Tate: You should go. Try and have a good time.

Willow: Not possible. I'd rather just go home after work.

Tate: Talk to you soon.

If Tate couldn't go with me, the obvious solution was to find a way out of it. It was still early, and I had all day to come up with an excuse to cancel. Dinner with Elizabeth was about as appetizing as swallowing nails. I might enjoy some time with Dad, but unfortunately the two of them came as a perfectly coiffed and manicured set. Oh well, I would think about that unpleasantness later.

Humming to myself, I unlocked the customer window and turned on the blinking Open sign. It wasn't long before the line began to form, snaking its way down the sidewalk. I never would have guessed that so many people would enjoy my food. The Dancing Crêpe's success had ignited a fire inside of me, and I couldn't wait to take things to the next level.

I worked methodically, ignoring the angry-sounding Russian words Katya spewed my way when she saw the long line at my window. She leaned out of her truck, shook her fist at me, and yelled something else. Trying not to make eye contact with the horrible woman next door, I whipped up crêpes as quickly as people ordered, smiling at new faces and making small talk with my regular customers. As was always the case when I was cooking, I became completely immersed in my work, and the concept of time just flew out the window.

Some people (namely my father) didn't understand my passion for food, but to me it was a calling. I loved the way that food could comfort and console on a bad day, and could make a good day even better. To me it was more than food; it was love on a plate.

I handed pirouettes (simple concoctions with powdered sugar and lemon curd) and relevés (savory crêpes with salmon and cream cheese) out the window all day long. Portlanders loved all things eccentric, and my ballet-themed crêpes fit the bill.

Glancing at my watch, I realized that the day had

completely gotten away from me; it was already six o'clock. I didn't have a set closing time, and basically finished up when I felt like it. Sometimes it was because I'd run out of ingredients; today was one of those days.

Reaching outside, I turned off the Open sign. After taking a few short minutes to tidy the cart and prepare for the next morning, I grabbed my phone. Rolling my eyes, I saw that there were six missed calls and two new voice mails. I angrily hit speakerphone and listened to my stepmother's nasal voice, which gave me the exact same sensation as fingernails being raked down a chalkboard.

"Willow, darling, your father is anxious to see you tonight. I hope you will think twice if you're planning to cancel as you usually do. He'll be devastated. Ciao, love." I growled in exasperation as I deleted the message.

Clicking Play on the next voice mail, I heard my father's booming voice through the speaker. "Willow, Elizabeth tells me you're screening your calls and refuse to answer. I hope you are planning to show up for dinner tonight. Your stepmother has gone to a lot of trouble with the reservations. You'll break her heart if you don't show."

Throwing my phone out the window of the food truck seemed like a perfectly reasonable reaction, but I stopped myself. Seeing my father and Elizabeth together was almost more than I could handle, so of course I'd planned to cancel. That was a given. But somehow, in the hustle and bustle of the day, I'd forgotten to come up with a good excuse. Now it was too late. I was scheduled to meet them in thirty minutes, exactly the amount of time it would take me to hop on a bus, drop Omelet off at home, and get across town.

As much as I would rather lay my naked flesh on the hot griddle I was cleaning, I knew there was no getting out of it. To make matters worse, I wouldn't even have time to clean myself up and change into "appropriate" dinner attire. I pictured the scathing look Elizabeth would send my way when I showed up at the fancy restaurant in my leggings, oversized sweater, and leopard-print rain boots. At that point, there was nothing I could do about it. If they were so anxious to see me, they would take me the way I was. Honestly, I sort of enjoyed the fact that my clothes would irritate Elizabeth. Getting under her skin—the way she did mine—was one of my favorite pastimes.

I secured Omelet's rain jacket, locked up the food truck, pulled my large hood over my head, and stepped outside into the pouring rain. Next door, Katya and one of her workers glared and yelled something at me as I passed by. I just smiled and waved, not really sure what else to do. Her anger was something to which I'd grown accustomed.

We walked around the block and arrived at the bus stop at exactly the same time as the bus. Climbing inside, I smiled at the driver and took my seat, placing Omelet on my lap. The bus sped down the busy streets, its headlights glistening off the puddles as we splashed through them. I watched out the window as blurry buildings and pedestrians passed by.

Shaking my head in wonder, I peered at the herd of bicyclists pedaling down the street, oblivious to the fact that they were riding around in the middle of a downpour. I couldn't imagine being that dedicated. I didn't even like to ride a bike in the sunshine. Of course, that was probably because I didn't like the sun all that much either. Since I was fair-skinned and red-haired, the sun was not my friend; we had been mortal enemies since my birth. I didn't tan; my freckles simply connected and I burned to the color of a lobster in a matter of minutes. Luckily, around here, it was cloudy nine months out of the year. The other three months I stayed inside.

Omelet and I jumped off at the stop near my apartment. I quickly hopped on the elevator, rode up to my floor, unlocked the door, hurried her out of her raincoat, and shooed her inside. She gave me an angry look when she realized I wasn't joining her. "I'll be home soon. I promise I'll fix your dinner then. I don't have time to stop now. You know how Elizabeth is… just awful." I wrinkled up my nose and Omelet just looked at me. She wasn't buying my excuse. I'd have some serious making up to do when I returned. But it couldn't be helped. I didn't need another reason to get on Dad's bad side.

I rushed back outside, hopped back on the bus, and rode until I arrived at the stop nearest the Eatery, one of Portland's finest restaurants. The Eatery was the kind of place that was always busy. Unless one had connections, it was nearly impossible to get a table. However, I learned early in life that the last name of Simpson opened doors that would otherwise be slammed in one's face. It was something I had come to accept, even though the preferential treatment always made me uncomfortable.

Here we go. I sighed heavily, smiled at the doorman as he

opened the ornate glass door, stepped inside onto the plush red carpet, and scanned the crowd for Dad and Elizabeth. It didn't take long to spot them. Elizabeth's voice floated above the din of the crowd, like a foghorn. I rolled my eyes dramatically, dreading the task at hand. *Why does being a good daughter have to be so difficult?*

Cringing, I prayed that I could keep my temper in check throughout dinner. Outwardly, I pasted on a serene expression and snaked my way through the tables, reaching the dreaded destination all too soon. When I saw my father, my heart constricted with sadness at his current state in life.

I'm not sure why it bothered me so much, when he didn't seem at all fazed by it; his shallow existence disturbed me on a very deep level though. Even if our relationship wasn't perfect, I loved him and truly wanted him to find some semblance of happiness. Then again, maybe the problem was mine. Maybe Dad was perfectly content with his life. After all, I wasn't exactly a relationship expert.

He often told me that I took after my mom, with my high ideals and Bohemian world view. I certainly didn't take after him. Although I had few memories of Mom, it always warmed my heart to hear Dad talk about our similarities. His memories were all I had left of her.

My mother, Fern Wolf Tremaine, was a fiery-haired, free-spirited young woman who grew up in a Kansas commune. A self-proclaimed hippie, she traveled to the Pacific Northwest to explore and find herself. She landed in Portland with nothing but her guitar and ten dollars to her name.

According to Dad, on Mom's first day in the city she was daydreaming and stepped into the busy street right in front of an oncoming car. It could have been a story with a terrible ending, but instead it was a modern-day fairy tale.

Dad, who was on his way to a business meeting, was walking behind her at the time. He saw the oncoming car and realized immediately that my mother hadn't noticed it. He thwarted the impending accident by scooping Mom right off the street and quickly whisking her to safety. Worlds collided, and the two strangers with absolutely nothing in common were drawn together like magnets.

My mother and father were inseparable from that moment, and they were married only two months later. Mom was the shining light and center of Dad's world. A few blissful years later, I was born. Our little family lived a nearly picture-perfect existence for the next five years, until Mom was taken away from us by ovarian cancer.

Something in my father died the day he buried my mother. It took him nearly a year before he could even look at me. His heart turned cold with Mom's death, and he told me he would never love anyone again. Although I couldn't remember much about her, I did remember that she loved us, and I also knew she would want me to take care of Dad. The loss of my mom was a constant ache in my soul; it left a gaping hole that nothing could fill.

Marrying her was the best decision my father ever made. He told me once that she was his soul mate and there would never be another true love for him in this lifetime. That's probably why he chose to marry women who were beautiful, but to whom he had no real connection. He knew my mom was his one great love, so he wasn't even trying to find another one.

Other than my parents', all the relationships I'd witnessed growing up were superficial, so I decided a long time ago that the pretense was something I could do without. I knew they'd had something great, but I had a hard time believing it could happen to other people. Their love story was a fluke; I was sure of it. I'd told Tate I was damaged goods, and I knew it was the truth. I'd managed to sabotage every relationship I'd ever had. I was a pessimist, and that was something Tate could do without, although I hadn't yet convinced him of that.

"Willow, are you planning to sit down?" Dad cleared his throat loudly, pulling me from my reverie and firmly back into the present. He and Elizabeth looked at me expectantly, and I wondered how long I'd been standing there daydreaming. From the looks on their faces, it had been far too long.

Dad was robust and dapper in his suit and tie, and he looked much younger than most fifty-five-year-old men. He was handsome and fit, and it was easy to see why he attracted young, beautiful women—even if you took his billions out of the picture. Elizabeth, whose slender hand clutched his possessively, was dressed to perfection in a little black number that probably cost more than the average person made in a year. The dress was accessorized by a sparkling diamond pendant the size of a golf ball. I was astonished that Elizabeth's tiny frame could support such a rock without toppling over. I imagined that the total carat weight of the necklace combined with the ostentatious wedding ring my father gave her was more than that of the woman herself.

"Daddy, hello." I leaned in and kissed my father on the cheek before seating myself across the table from him.

"We're so glad you could make it," Dad said as I settled in. "Aren't you going to greet Elizabeth?"

"I was just getting to that. It's good to see you too, Elizabeth." I pasted a fake smile on my face and tried not to choke on the words. "That necklace is dazzling. Isn't it heavy?"

"Your father just gave it to me this afternoon, for absolutely no reason. Can you believe what a sweetheart he is?" She turned her perfect face and fluttered her eyelashes at Dad, who absentmindedly patted her hand the way a parent pats a small child.

I could practically feel a cavity forming from all the fake sweetness spewing from Elizabeth's mouth. It was like a saccharine overdose. Instead of voicing the sarcastic remark that was just begging to be set free, I smiled and said, "That's so nice. Dad certainly knows how to keep a woman's attention."

"Just look at you, Willow. You look so... so... comfortable this evening. Did you come here straight from work?" Elizabeth practically spat the last word out, as if working for a living were more than she could stomach.

"I did, and I had a great day, thanks for asking. Working for a living is quite fulfilling. Not that you would know anything about that, of course." I smiled, refusing to allow the horrible woman to demean me. I was just about to say something even worse when I was interrupted by Dad, who obviously didn't trust me to keep my words in check. *The man knows me too well.*

"Willow, why don't you take a look at the menu? We've already decided what we're having." Dad handed the leather-bound book to me, a look of warning on his face.

Taking the menu obediently, I scanned the delicious choices before finally settling on the Columbia River steelhead. As a cook, I knew locally procured ingredients were always the best, and the fish was sure to be fresh.

When the server approached, we each ordered in turn. I rolled my eyes and barely suppressed a groan as Elizabeth asked for "the small side salad with no dressing, please." I was certain the bony woman would nibble on one piece of lettuce and announce that she was stuffed. *Ridiculous.*

An awkward silence settled over the table as we waited for our meals to arrive. I thought of a million things I would like to say, but every one of them was a slam on Elizabeth. Instead, I thought it best if I held my tongue unless spoken to. That might be easier said than done.

"So, honey, how is your little stand going?" Dad flicked his azure eyes in my direction. My hazel ones, exactly like my mother's, met his with determination.

"My little stand, as you put it, is doing extremely well. If sales continue the way they're going, I will have my restaurant in the next few years." I smiled proudly. It was the first real one since I'd sat down to this farce of a family dinner.

"That's fantastic, although completely unnecessary. You know, if you would just let me help you, it would all happen so much sooner," Dad said indulgently.

"I don't want your help, Dad," I snapped; my voice sounded much more abrasive than I intended. Taking a deep breath and trying again, I continued, "I mean, this is really something I want to do on my own, without your help. You understand, right?"

"Not really, but I'll respect your wishes. You know, there's nothing wrong with taking help from your father. No one else seems to have a problem taking what I'm willing to give." Dad's eyes darted in Elizabeth's direction quickly, and I thought I detected some animosity behind his words. *Is there trouble in paradise already?* A girl could dream.

"I know, Dad, but really, I want to do this alone. I appreciate the offer, but please, let's just change the subject. Let's talk about something else. What have you two been doing lately?" I attempted to bring Elizabeth into the conversation, and felt that I deserved an award for how kind I was being. Unfortunately, she didn't even notice. My stepmother was staring off into the distance, a concerned look on her face.

"Elizabeth?" Dad spoke loudly to his wife, and she jumped.

"What? Oh… sorry… were you talking to me?" she stammered as her icy eyes darted back and forth between Dad and me.

"Yes. Willow asked what we've been up to lately," Dad prompted his visibly frazzled young wife.

"Oh… well… you know… just the usual. I've been spending some time at the country club, shopping, lunching, tennis, working out with my personal trainer, planning the upcoming Fireman's Ball. Nothing new." She tapped her manicured fingernail on the table, her agitation completely obvious.

"Elizabeth, is anything wrong?" I was certain that something was not quite right with her tonight. Normally, she was just incredibly condescending and annoying. Tonight, she seemed agitated and anxious.

"Of course nothing is wrong. Why would it be? I have a perfect life!" Elizabeth's voice rose an octave and her hands fluttered to her chest, where she nervously fingered the gargantuan diamond necklace.

If Dad noticed his wife's strange behavior, he didn't comment. Instead, he was busy glancing at his cell phone, probably checking on Simpson Coffee's stocks. As always, he was oblivious. It was the story of my life.

Thankfully, the food arrived. I was never so glad to have something to do with my hands. The food was also a good excuse not to talk, since I'd racked my brain to come up with something nice to say and come up empty.

All I wanted was to finish the agonizing meal and go home, but as uncomfortable as I was with my dinner companions, I was completely blown away by the Eatery's food. A true artist created it, and I ate my steelhead with admiration, savoring each delectable bite.

As soon as we were done, Elizabeth excused herself, saying she had to make a phone call. Dad and I sat quietly, the stream of conversation drying up like the Sahara Desert. After several uncomfortable moments of silence, I decided I'd done my duty and put in my time. I was more than ready to go home and feed my starving cat.

"Thanks for dinner, Dad. I need to get home now. It's been a long day, and Omelet will be waiting for food." I could already see the judgmental look I was going to get from my finicky feline for feeding her so late.

Scooting my chair away from the table, I stood to leave. Dad paid the tab and walked me to the front door. We saw Elizabeth, who was standing outside talking on her phone; her back was turned, so she didn't see us approaching. She spoke loudly; whoever was on the other end of the line had certainly incurred her wrath.

I was only able to catch the tail end of the conversation, but it was something to the tune of, "I don't care how you do it. I gave you everything you need. Just get it done. That's what I paid you for!"

She ended the call and angrily shoved her cell phone into her Prada handbag before pivoting on her Christian Louboutin heels. Her face registered surprise when she saw us standing there, but she composed herself quickly and pasted on a syrupy smile as she said, "That was the landscaper. I swear, some people just cannot follow the simplest instructions."

I couldn't imagine what it would be like to work for my wicked stepmother, and I decided that was my cue to exit stage left. I hugged my father quickly, nodded curtly to Elizabeth, and headed on my way. I finally felt as if I could breathe again as I put some distance between us.

Chapter Four

Fresh air was a necessity after the uncomfortable meal, so I opted to walk the half mile to my apartment rather than jump on the bus. Walking briskly toward home, I replayed the disastrous dinner in my mind. I couldn't believe Dad had willingly entangled himself with that terrible woman. Sure, Elizabeth was undeniably beautiful, but I had a hard time believing that my stepmother's good looks could in any way make up for her lack of personality and charm; not to mention the fact that she was incredibly boring. She had no hobbies besides shopping and lunching with her friends, who were every bit as vapid as she was.

I knew she was only after Dad's money, and I couldn't believe my father couldn't see that for himself. I hoped he'd made her sign a prenuptial agreement before the wedding. I knew he had with all of his other wives, but he was different with Elizabeth. She had probably convinced him that it wasn't necessary. Then again, maybe he just had so much money that he didn't care if he lost some. For an intelligent man, my father was stupid when it came to women.

I was nearly home when I had the strangest sensation of being followed. It started as a tingling on the back of my neck and crept along inside me like a snake. It was unnerving. I picked up the pace, glancing behind me. Although I didn't see anyone, the feeling wouldn't go away.

I continued to my apartment at a fast pace, looking furtively behind me as I walked. The nagging feeling of being watched continued to gnaw at me. Some things a girl just knows in her gut, and that was one of them. I slipped my key into the outer door of my apartment building and hurried quickly inside, yanking the door closed behind me and jiggling the knob. Sometimes the latch didn't catch right and it blew open. Breathing a sigh of relief that I was safe, I hopped on the elevator and rode to the fourth floor.

My building was certainly not one of the poshest ones in Portland, but it wasn't the worst one either. Dad had offered to put me up in the swankiest building in the Pearl District, and he'd even insisted on paying my rent, but I'd declined. I didn't want to live with rich people. I'd done that my entire life. I just wanted a normal apartment building. I didn't want a handout. So, I'd compromised, choosing instead a decent building that I could actually afford on the fringes of the Pearl District. It was a safe enough neighborhood, in my opinion.

Dad guilted me into believing that he would rest easier if

he knew my building was secure, and I'd assured him that it was. Of course, I'd left out the part about the front door not closing all the way, and the fact that there had been a few robberies in the building since I'd moved in. It didn't make sense for him to worry any more than he already did. In spite of its quirks, I loved my apartment. It was spacious, well-lit, and had a fantastic fireplace. The best part about it was that it was all mine.

Exiting the elevator, I walked down the tiled hallway to my apartment. Slipping the key into the lock, I opened the door and went inside. As always, I flipped on all the lights as I entered; it was a habit. I hated walking into a dark room. I dropped my purse and keys on the small table in the foyer, kicked off my soggy rain boots, and hung up my coat. I was just about to flip the deadbolt when I heard Omelet meowing in the other room, and from the sound of things, I was definitely in trouble for being late.

"I'll be right there, Omelet," I called.

After a long day at work and a laborious dinner with Dad and Elizabeth, I was in desperate need of a hot shower; but first, I needed to heat up the chilliness of my apartment. I flipped on the switch that ignited the fire in the gas fireplace, and headed into my bedroom.

The rest of my house was neat as a pin, but my bedroom was the polar opposite. Clothing was strewn all over the beige carpet. The computer desk in the corner of my room had papers piled haphazardly upon it. My large bed remained unmade, and the lavender silk sheets beckoned. To the average onlooker, it would appear that there was no rhyme or reason to the chaos, but I had the uncanny ability to find anything in the room in a matter of seconds.

My bedroom was my sanctuary; it was the one place in my home that I didn't mind being messy. Besides, I was the only one who ever saw it, other than Tate and Omelet, and they didn't care what it looked like.

Stepping into the adjoining bathroom, I turned on the shower as hot as it would go. I felt chilled to the bone from my walk home, not to mention the fact that I was still spooked about being followed. It was strange that I hadn't seen anyone behind me when my intuition screamed that someone was there. It must have been my mind playing tricks on me; I was just stressed out and my nerves were on edge.

I'd been working nonstop, and I was worried about injuring my friendship with Tate because of his big revelation. I'd even been having strange dreams about my best friend. The latest one had featured a beautifully elegant wedding where I was the bride and he was the groom. I'd awakened from that little gem drenched with sweat and hyperventilating. Throw in the horror of having to deal with Elizabeth, and my sanity had obviously reached its limit. That had to be it. I couldn't change my workload, or the fact that I had to walk a fine line with Tate, but I did need to figure out a way to stop thinking about Elizabeth.

As a general rule, I considered myself an easygoing girl. True, I was a tad emotional, and I tended to overthink nearly everything. I was pretty impulsive, and I could be a bit irrational, but it was virtually impossible for most people to offend me. Elizabeth managed to do so with her very existence. Since the moment I'd met her, way back in elementary school, my nice streak took a hike as far as she was concerned. Every single thing about her irritated and angered me. I realized my feelings were probably blown out of proportion, but it was the way I felt and I couldn't help it.

When Dad had told me they were getting married, I begged and pleaded with him to reconsider. When that didn't work, I threw a tantrum that would put a two-year-old to shame. I screamed and yelled, calling my father every name in the book; I even threw a Waterford crystal vase across the room, shattering a large plate-glass window in the process. It certainly wasn't my proudest moment, but I did what I felt was necessary. Dad hadn't been swayed by my immature, dramatic behavior; in fact, he moved the wedding up by two months just to spite me.

As a last resort, I gave my father the silent treatment and told him that I refused to attend his sham of a wedding. After a few weeks though, I felt guilty about all of it and gave in. I begrudgingly went to the wedding, although I drew the line at smiling for the photographs. My obvious displeasure about the event was apparent for all to see in Dad and Elizabeth's fancy leather-bound wedding album. I didn't feel guilty about that at all. Besides, this marriage wouldn't last any longer than the other ones had.

And there I was, still thinking about her. "Enough, Willow," I scolded myself.

Turning off the faucet, I stepped out of the shower into

the steamy bathroom to dry off, wrapping one fluffy bath towel around my slender frame and twisting another into a turban over my red curls. I padded softly into the bedroom to get my pajamas. That's when I saw Omelet sitting on the bed, looking at me disapprovingly with her cat-green eyes. I'd completely forgotten to feed her and felt like the worst cat mom ever. The hypercritical feline sat licking her fluffy gray fur, probably wishing it was fish.

"Sorry, baby. I'll go feed you right now. Come on," I cooed to Omelet, who yawned, stretched, and hopped off the bed before disdainfully following me into the kitchen.

I opened the pantry and poured food into her dish, mixing in a spoonful of tuna as a peace offering. Omelet looked at me contentedly, and I was relieved to be momentarily forgiven. While she ate, I went into the living room, happy I'd turned on the fireplace before taking a shower. The flickering flames warmed the room, and I placed myself directly in front of them, then unwound the towel on my head and let my wet hair tumble down my back. I finger combed my curls and sat on the floor next to the fire, allowing them to dry more quickly. I sighed contentedly, thinking this was the perfect way to end my stressful day.

My body was warm, in spite of the fact that I was only wrapped in my bath towel. I knew I should probably go get dressed, but the heat from the fireplace was making me feel lazy. So instead, I grabbed a pillow from the couch and placed it under my head, fanning my hair out on top of it to dry.

I stretched out on the floor, closed my eyes, and basked

in the blessed silence. I had the fleeting thought that I would most likely fall asleep right there, but I was so comfortable that it didn't even matter. The ability to do exactly as I pleased was one of the many perks of living alone.

Somewhere between waking and sleeping, I heard Omelet meow. I groaned and tried to ignore her, certain that I must be dreaming. She meowed again and again, which wasn't like her at all. I reluctantly decided I should check on my cat, but all I really wanted to do was sleep. Being a pet parent was a demanding job.

When I opened my eyes, my entire body seized with terror, going from sleepiness to high alert. I didn't see Omelet anywhere. What I saw instead was a giant of a man, dressed completely in black, his face strategically hidden by a ski mask. He towered over me holding the butcher knife from my own kitchen. From personal experience, I knew the implement was quite sharp, and I had no desire to become intimately acquainted with it.

Unfortunately, my sense of self-preservation seemed to be on vacation. I was completely frozen in fear, unable to move for what seemed like years. The giant didn't move either, and I wondered why. Strangely enough, he seemed just as surprised as I was that he was in my living room. We looked at each other, his beady eyes visible through the holes of his ski mask. The synapses in my brain finally began to fire, and I jumped into action, kicking the intruder as hard as I could in the groin. He groaned in pain and clumsily took a swipe at me with the knife as he sank to his knees.

I rolled out of his path and jumped swiftly to my feet.

Unfortunately, the maneuver didn't work exactly as I planned. I lost my towel in the process and was startled to remember that I was completely naked underneath. My lack of clothing was the least of my worries. I had far bigger fish to fry.

I darted into the kitchen and ducked behind the counter. He rose slowly and lumbered toward me. *Think, Willow, think!*

The man was huge, larger than any human I'd ever seen. I made a quick mental note that his terrifying size might also work against him. Conversely, I was small and quick, and I was determined to use those things to my advantage. I didn't have much else. As he drew close to me, I sprinted back into the living room. Until I figured out what to do next, I had to stay out of his way.

To be honest, I didn't have much to offer in the strength department, and I fleetingly wished that I would have paid more attention to weight training at some point in my life. There was no time for regrets at that moment though, so I took quick stock of what I could use to fight back. There was a large paperweight on the table in the foyer. If I could get to that, I could smash him in the head with it. Of course, if I managed to get that far, I'd be better off running out the front door. I thought about my ballet classes and made a list of moves I could use for self-defense. Granted, it wasn't much, but it was all I had.

A grand battement might do the trick. I could bring my foot right up to his face and take him out, with my toes perfectly pointed of course. Given his size though, I doubted if my foot would reach that far. I groaned, wishing I had some martial arts experience instead. Ballet wasn't exactly famous for its self-defense tactics, but it would have to do. Rich girls weren't brought up to fight intruders. That's what Dad paid the bodyguards to do.

I jumped behind the couch, thankful that there was at least a large piece of furniture between me and the colossus. I was hopeful that one of my neighbors might overhear the altercation, although I knew that was a long shot. I could die there and no one would know until some unlucky neighbor smelled my rotting flesh from the hallway.

"Who are you? What do you want?" I tried my best to sound intimidating, although I highly doubted the man would fear a skinny, naked girl with half-dried frizzy red curls whose only form of self-defense was ballet.

"What do I want?" The hulking man actually threw his head back and laughed at me. "I'm going to kill you."

"No, you're not. You can't just come into my home and kill me. That's rude!" I realized how stupid the words sounded as soon as I said them. He was hardly a man who was concerned with proper protocol. He obviously made a living at being rude.

"You're a little spitfire, aren't you? My boss told me you might give me some trouble. She said not to let you talk too much." The man, who spoke with an accent, brandished the knife as he moved closer to me.

"She? Who's she? Who's your boss?" I was far more interested in what the man had to say than I should have been.

A smarter woman would be running for her life, not exchanging conversation. Apparently, I wasn't as intelligent as I liked to think, because I continued to ask questions. "Who told you I was a spitfire? I mean, I suppose it's true. Actually, it's sort of a compliment, but that's beside the point."

The man laughed again and shook his head. *What a strange intruder he was!* Before I knew what was happening, he reached across the couch, grabbed me by the arm, and dragged my body over the cushions, knocking over the large piece of furniture in the process. His brute strength was really quite impressive. I watched as the man's bulging biceps rippled through his skintight black shirt. *Nice muscles.* He obviously worked out.

Shaking my head, I reminded myself that now was not the time to admire my attacker. Now was the time to stay focused, which was unfortunately not my strong suit. My body thudded to the ground along with the couch, and I groaned in pain. I would have taken off running, but the man retained his iron grip on my arm. *That's going to leave a bruise.*

"Let me go!" I firmly reprimanded the giant as I wriggled on the ground, trying my hardest to break free from his mammoth grip. It was the equivalent of a gnat flying repeatedly into an elephant; it made no impact whatsoever.

"You sure are a funny little thing, and pretty too. It's a shame I have to do this." The man raised the knife above me. I was officially running out of options, but I knew I had to do something, and fast.

With all the strength I had, I slammed my elbow straight into his shin. I felt the pointy bone make contact and hit its mark, and the giant dropped my arm. The knife fell from his hand and bounced on the carpet as the man wrapped both of his hands around his leg and howled. He groaned and spewed a string of obscenities in some other language. Now I'd done it; I'd really awakened the beast.

I jumped to my feet and ran across the room as quickly as I could. Unfortunately for me, the man's recovery time was faster than I expected; he grabbed me by my hair and yanked me roughly toward him. My assailant's anger was palpable. I had a momentary vision of the Incredible Hulk turning green and ripping through his clothing, but I reminded myself not to get distracted. *Again.*

"Please, don't hurt me. I know you don't want to do this," I pleaded, attempting to diffuse the bomb that was about to explode. I saw a flicker of regret in his dark eyes, and he sighed loudly.

"Enough talking!" the giant said as he towered over me. "You're dead now." He raised the butcher knife above his head, and although I knew he intended to kill me, I also sensed his hesitation. He didn't seem nearly as angry as he had a moment ago.

"You know, I think we got off on the wrong foot. You don't want to hurt me." I tried to appeal to his humanity, if he had any.

"I don't want to, but I have to. I promised her, and besides, I already took the money. She will kill me if I don't kill you." He scratched his head through the ski mask, appearing to contemplate what he should say next. As he was ruminating on his lot in life, I kicked him in the stomach with all my strength, knocking the wind out of him, and scrambled to my feet.

The man doubled over in pain, and I kicked him again, this time in the side. Instinctively, he flailed the knife around madly as he struggled to catch his breath. The sharp blade made contact, slicing into the flesh of my arm, but I didn't care. I had to get out of there.

I sprinted to the front door, grasping frantically for the door knob. The man straightened and lumbered toward me. I threw open the door and ran down the hallway, screaming and banging desperately on the first door I saw. I had no idea who lived there, and I prayed that someone was home. Stark naked and bloody was definitely not an ideal way to meet one's neighbors, but I was left with no choice.

The door opened, and without even acknowledging the person who answered, I pushed my way inside as I saw the intruder disappear into the emergency stairwell down the hall.

"Help… please… that man… he attacked me," I panted as I flailed my arms and tried to point at the stairway.

The person who answered the door barely hesitated before blasting off like a rocket in a dead run after the intruder. I gasped for air, on the verge of hyperventilating because of the ordeal I'd narrowly escaped, knowing my lungs would never feel full again. My head spun wildly, and nausea flooded me. I reached out to grab the wall for support, but felt myself falling in slow motion.

Chapter Five

"Wake up… open your eyes. Can you hear me?"

I heard a strange voice in the distance, but I felt like I was underwater, deep down near the ocean floor, struggling as hard as I could to make it to the surface. I forced my eyes open and looked around frantically, uncertain where I was. Nothing around was familiar, except for the handsome face that was only inches away from mine. *This is not happening. Please, tell me this isn't happening.*

I jumped up from the floor and immediately experienced a terrible head rush. Reaching out instinctively, I grabbed the man for support. All at once, the events from earlier came crashing into my memory, along with the realization that I was completely naked.

"It's you." I awkwardly tried to cover my body with my hands.

"Yes, it's me," replied Marcus, the sexy man from the coffee shop. I'd sworn I was going to avoid him, and I'd been successful. Until that moment.

He reached over and grabbed a fleece blanket that was folded neatly on the nearby leather couch. With gentle hands, he wrapped it around my body, which was shivering uncontrollably. He led me to the kitchen, where he calmly helped me into a chair.

"You're injured, and you're probably in shock, but if you are able to, I need you to try and remember what happened." Marcus strode purposefully across the kitchen and opened a cupboard.

He grabbed gauze, sterile pads, and a cloth, which he heated with steaming water. While I watched him move, fragments of what just happened in my apartment began to force their way into my brain.

"I… don't really remember. There was a man… in my apartment. He tried to kill me," I stammered as the events began to come into focus.

Pulling the blanket off my shoulder, he gingerly placed the warm cloth on my arm, applying gentle pressure to the knife wound I noticed at that very moment. The blood flow had basically stopped, but from the looks of things, I'd lost my fair share. Embarrassed, I realized that there was a puddle of blood at the front door.

"I'm so sorry. I got blood all over your house. I didn't realize I was bleeding." I glanced up into the kind eyes of the man I now realized was my neighbor.

He was tall, probably more than six feet, and had beautiful

brown eyes that looked like pools of melted chocolate. His dark hair was cut very short, but I could tell there was a hint of wave to it. His chiseled features and muscular physique brought to mind a Greek god. I swallowed nervously, unable to believe that he had been next door to me all along and I hadn't had a clue.

"Don't worry about the blood. The important thing is that you're safe." He looked at me, and my stomach flip-flopped.

I was desperately trying to forget the fact that the first time we'd met I'd run headfirst into a glass door, and this time I was naked and bleeding. *You haven't exactly made a great impression, Willow.* Nevertheless, he smiled at me, and his whole face lit up. Straight, perfect white teeth stood like soldiers at attention. The man was as exquisite as I remembered.

"Well, I'm sorry I barged into your home and bled all over it. I didn't know what else to do, and I'm glad you were here. I can't imagine what might have happened to me if you didn't answer your door." I shivered at the truth in my words.

From Marcus's living room, I heard a plaintive meow, and Omelet trotted into the kitchen, a worried expression on her little cat face. I deduced that Omelet must have followed my blood trail to find me. My cat was a genius, a regular Omelet, PI.

"This little one belongs to you, right? I remember her from the coffee shop. I'd never seen a cat drink a latte before." Marcus placed the cloth on the table and bent down to scoop up my cat.

I was just about to warn him not to touch her, but I wasn't fast enough. Omelet wasn't a fan of strangers, particularly men. The only man she liked was Tate, and that was only because she'd known him all her life.

Squeezing my eyes shut, I waited for Marcus to howl in pain as Omelet made her man-hating tendencies known. To my surprise, the only sound I heard was a happy purr, and I opened my eyes to see her settled contentedly in Marcus's arms.

"Are you some kind of cat whisperer? Omelet doesn't like strangers." I stared in wonder as she nuzzled Marcus happily.

"I think she's an excellent judge of character." Marcus smiled as he gently placed her on my lap. Omelet licked my face happily.

"I'm sure you don't remember, since you passed out, but I ran after the guy. Is he someone you know?" Marcus eyed me, waiting for my answer.

"No. I assure you, I've never seen that man before in my life. I fell asleep on my living room floor and when I opened my eyes, he was standing there with the butcher knife from my kitchen. He had on a ski mask, so I have no idea what he looks like, but I can guarantee you, I'll know him if I ever see him again. I'll never forget his eyes. I think he followed me home. He told me he was going to kill me… that he had to because he'd already taken the money, whatever that meant. He kept referring to his boss. I fought back and then ran to your door. I'm afraid I don't know any more than that." I took a shuddering breath as I quickly summed up the awful ordeal.

"The goon had a head start on me, or I would have caught him. He took off his mask, and I got a good look at his face when he turned around though. I would recognize him if I saw him again." Marcus's jaw was set determinedly, and I had no doubt that my obviously buff neighbor would have taken the man down if he'd caught up to him.

"You managed to get close enough to see his face? That's pretty amazing. He had to be nearly all the way to the ground floor by the time you started. Are you an Olympic sprinter?" I stared at Marcus, unable to conceal my admiration.

"Close, I'm a police officer," he replied.

"Of course you are. Well, that comes in handy." I couldn't believe my luck. I had managed to stumble into my gorgeous neighbor's apartment, cut and bleeding from an attack, and he just so happened to be a police officer. What were the odds? "Does that mean I can skip the whole filing a police report thing? I can just tell you, right?"

Marcus chuckled as if I'd said something funny. "It doesn't really work that way, Willow. I've already called the station, and they're sending out an officer to investigate. They'll need to go through your apartment to see if there's any evidence. They should be here soon."

"Oh, okay. That sounds very official." I swallowed hard, uncomfortable with the idea of having to relive the event all over again.

"Not to worry, I'll be right beside you." Marcus finished patching up my arm, which was stinging like mad.

I couldn't help but notice that for someone so strong, Marcus had extremely gentle hands, and that sent my mind down a rabbit trail I hadn't expected. I wondered what other things those gentle hands were good at. Then I scolded myself for having thoughts like that. I'd just been attacked, for goodness sake! I had far more important things to worry about than my extremely attractive neighbor and his gentle hands.

Omelet decided she wanted to explore and jumped off my lap. I hoped she'd avoid the blood trail. Bathing her was not something I wanted to tackle on top of everything else.

Marcus said I wouldn't need stitches, although he did imply that the cut was pretty deep and I should keep a close eye on it. I knew I was lucky that I'd escaped with only a minor injury. The idea started to sink in that someone broke into my home and tried to kill me, someone obviously hired by a person I knew.

Tears welled up in my eyes. They blinded me and threatened to spill out. I fought them back. I would not cry in front of Marcus. The man certainly thought I was a complete mental case already.

I sat there blinking back the tears. I tried my best to think of other things to divert my mind, but now that the shock was gone, the memories of what happened came rushing back. As hard as I tried not to cry, the floodgates opened anyway. Tears started to drop, one by one at first, and then like a waterfall. I began to sob uncontrollably—an ugly cry, where the snot and tears mixed together to create one horrific mess.

Instead of looking uncomfortable as men often do when women cry, Marcus pulled me close to him and wrapped his strong arms around my shaking body. Someone had obviously trained this man properly. I felt safe in his embrace, so I didn't pull away, even though he was a complete stranger. I had the fleeting thought that Marcus must be a good guy or Omelet wouldn't like him. I trusted my cat's judgment implicitly.

I continued to sob, holding nothing back, until my tears ran dry. Marcus grabbed another wet cloth and tenderly wiped my face. He smiled and wrapped his arms around me again, smoothed my hair, and whispered comforting words into my ear. It was by far one of the most surreal moments of my life.

Strangely, I didn't feel embarrassed about breaking down in front of him though. My reaction to the whole situation was very abnormal. The fact that I was an emotional mess wasn't unusual. That was par for the course in my world. The strange part was the fact that I felt comfortable with a man I barely knew. Normally, it took a very long time for that to happen. Marcus had such a genuine, caring way about him though. He put me at ease. Rather than question it, I rested my head on his chest and allowed myself to just be held and comforted.

I wasn't a big hugger—besides Tate, of course—and I'd always thought physical closeness was overrated, but in Marcus's arms, I knew I'd been wrong about that. Apparently hugging wasn't so bad. Even more confusing was the fact that I was enjoying it far more than I should have been, given I knew virtually nothing at all about the person holding me.

I tentatively lifted my head off Marcus's chest and looked up at his face. Our eyes locked, but instead of breaking contact as I normally would, I discovered that I couldn't tear my gaze away. I was shocked and terrified to realize that I wanted to kiss him. I was obviously in the middle of a breakdown. There was no other reasonable explanation.

What's come over me? Maybe it was the shock of the dangerous situation I'd just escaped. Whatever the reasons for my sudden personality shift, I knew I couldn't follow through with kissing a stranger. But even though I didn't plaster my face to his like I wanted to, I couldn't seem to stop looking at him, and strangely enough, he seemed to be having the same problem. *Willow Simpson, you've officially lost your mind.*

The moment was shattered by the sound of the buzzer. Startled by the noise, I pulled away and looked at Marcus questioningly. With my luck, it was probably his girlfriend.

"I'm… sorry. I don't usually hug… strangers… like that," I stammered in explanation.

"It takes two." Marcus smiled widely, letting me know he wasn't completely appalled by my lack of decorum.

"The door." I pointed toward it.

"That will be the officer from the local precinct. He'll want to talk to both of us," Marcus explained, as he pushed the button to open the door to the building.

He led the officer into the kitchen. The gray-haired policeman, Officer Peterson, smiled politely and apologized for the trauma I had experienced. With the pleasantries out of the way, he jumped right in with questions. I told him everything I could remember, which honestly wasn't much. Marcus gave his statement as well and filled in a few of the things that I'd left out.

"Is there anyone you can think of who might want to hurt you?" questioned the officer.

"No! Of course not! Why would anyone want to hurt me?" I was appalled by the invasive question.

"Well, miss, in my experience with assault cases, it usually leads back to someone the victim knows," he explained.

"Well, I told you that he said some woman hired him, so it's obviously a female that I know. But I can't think of anyone who would want me dead," I assured him.

Officer Peterson nodded and informed me that we all had to take a trip next door to my apartment to survey the "crime scene." I didn't like having my home referred to in that way, but unfortunately, I supposed that's what it was.

Marcus helped me to secure the fleece blanket, which was the only thing standing between me and an arrest for indecent exposure. I was still quite naked underneath. Omelet, probably wondering what exciting thing was going to happen next, trailed behind us as we left Marcus's apartment. We followed Officer Peterson, who entered first to be sure it was secure. Once we got the green light, we all went inside.

I shivered as I surveyed the disaster that was my home. Marcus patted my back comfortingly. A trail of what I could only assume was my own blood zigzagged from the living room floor to the front door, and then led down the hallway to Marcus's door. About that time, a forensics team arrived and began to look around for evidence. I watched as they took a few samples of the blood, and I agreed when they asked for a swab of my DNA to confirm whether all of the blood was mine, or if some of it might be the attacker's.

The group of police professionals spoke in hushed voices, scribbled notes into official-looking files, put things into plastic bags, and scoured my entire apartment for clues. I just stood there, cowering in the corner like a scared rabbit, clothed in nothing but the bloodstained blanket that belonged to my neighbor. It really didn't get any more surreal than that.

My couch was tipped over, and the cushions were strewn about the room. The coffee table was toppled on its side. I honestly couldn't remember how it got that way, but it probably happened when the man pulled me across the couch. Officer Peterson eyed the damage with a frustrated look on his face. Then he bent down to pick up a piece of paper that was lying on the floor next to the chair. I hadn't noticed it before.

"Is this yours?" He showed me a torn slip of paper with a phone number written on it.

I examined the paper and decided that the phone number looked familiar. At that moment, I couldn't recall whose number it was. I did my best to remember the digits, knowing I would need to look through my contacts later for clues.

"No, that's not my writing." I shook my head. "Maybe the intruder dropped it?"

"Maybe. Don't worry, we'll check it out and find out whose it is." The officer placed the piece of paper into a plastic bag and continued looking around the room. Instead of assisting the team as I assumed he would, Marcus stayed right beside me, his arm wrapped securely around my shoulders. It made me feel safe as I digested the chaos in my living room.

The forensics team finished their investigation. Officer Peterson made a few scribbles on the notepad in his hand, told Marcus he would be in touch, nodded at me, and left. I heard the front door close behind him, and just like that, Marcus and I were alone in my apartment.

"Now what?" I looked at Marcus, not sure what I was supposed to do next.

"Now I'm going to help you straighten up your living room. And don't worry, I won't leave you alone until they catch that guy," he answered.

"What if they don't?" I asked, suddenly very afraid.

"We will. I promise you," he assured me. "I have to make a phone call to the precinct. If it's all right with you, I'm going to volunteer to be part of your watch."

"My watch?" I had no idea what he meant.

"You're the target of a potential murder, Willow. You need someone to watch out for you. I would be more than willing to be that person, as long as you want me to be," Marcus explained.

"You mean the police station is going to pay you to be

my bodyguard?" I asked.

"Probably not. But I'm off for the next two days, and I will do it in my free time until we figure something else out," he answered quickly.

"No, Marcus, this isn't your problem. I'm practically a stranger. Why would you do that?"

"Honestly, I have no idea," he said with a laugh. "But I do feel like you're in danger, and I have the ability and the experience to protect you. Besides, you're my neighbor, and you have the coolest cat I've ever seen."

"I do have a pretty awesome cat." I smiled.

"Let's just play it by ear. I'll have a talk with my boss and see if we can get a permanent watch assigned to you. For now, I'm considering it my own personal mission to protect you," Marcus replied.

"Do you really think it's necessary?" I still wasn't convinced.

"Yes, Willow, I think it's entirely necessary," he answered.

"All right, if I need to be watched, I suppose it would be better if it was someone I sort of know." I couldn't imagine the thought of some stranger spending every minute with me, but if it were Marcus, it just might be okay.

"Is there anyone you need to call? Shouldn't you let a family member know what's happened?" Marcus suggested.

"Yeah, I probably should. I'll call my Dad, and I definitely need to call my best friend," I said.

"All right, I'll make a quick phone call to the station. You can make yours, and then we will get started on cleaning up this mess. What do you say?"

"I say that I'm really glad that it was you who answered the door tonight. Thank you, Marcus," I answered.

I couldn't believe what I'd just been through. It was going to take me some time to sort through all the emotions and come to grips with everything, but I was really grateful that I had such a wonderful neighbor to help me through it.

Chapter Six

After showering the crusted blood from my body, I threw on yoga pants and an old T-shirt, grabbed a pile of blankets from the hall closet, and carried them into my living room. Depositing them on the couch, I looked questioningly at Marcus.

"You know, you really don't have to stay. I'm sure you would be much more comfortable in your own bed tonight." I hated being a burden on him. "Besides, I left a message for my Dad, and I'm sure he'll get back to me soon. My best friend will be calling on his break too. I'm not your responsibility."

"Willow, someone has to stay here with you. That thug knows where you live. He might come back in the middle of the night, and then what? Besides, I told you that I'm your official watch. This is my job. If you're worried about your virtue, you shouldn't be. I promise I'll stay on the couch." Marcus grinned, and I was sure he was attempting to lighten a very difficult situation.

Since there was nothing at all I could do about it, I decided I might as well play along. "Maybe it's not my virtue I'm worried about. Maybe it's yours. Did you ever think of that? I mean, who knows? *I* might take advantage of *you* in the middle of the night."

"I'm willing to take my chances." Marcus smiled again and my insides turned to mush.

If he kept this up, I just might tell him he didn't have to sleep on the couch at all. *Get a handle on yourself, woman!* The sound of my phone ringing on the kitchen counter startled us both.

"I better grab that." I reluctantly pulled my eyes away from Marcus and looked at the display on my phone. It was Tate.

I took a deep breath and tried to sound as normal as possible, given the fact that my heart was racing about a thousand miles per hour. "Hello?"

"Hey, babe, how was work? I got your message to call. What's up?" Tate's familiar voice on the other end of the phone brought tears to my eyes. I knew I had to tread lightly when I told him what had happened tonight. He tended to panic when it came to my safety.

"Work was good, but then I came home, and… well… there's something I need to tell you, but you have to promise not to freak out." I had no idea how to tell him the truth. He was so protective; I knew he would insist on rushing right over as soon as I broke the news.

"Freak out? Me? When is the last time I freaked out?" he demanded.

"Nearly every time you think something is wrong," I replied.

"That's because I care about you. Just tell me what happened."

"Someone broke into my house and tried to kill me." I decided there was only one way to get it out, so I blurted the words quickly, just like ripping off a Band-Aid.

"Someone tried to kill you? Willow, are you all right? Never mind, I'll be there in ten minutes. But I can't be there in ten minutes. I'm at work." The frustration in his voice was apparent.

"Just hold up, Tate. I'm fine. The intruder is gone, and all he left me with was a little scratch." I decided to downplay the severity of my injuries. Marcus, who was sitting next to me on a barstool, listening to the conversation, raised one eyebrow at my obvious lie.

"He might be gone now, but what if he comes back? You can't be there alone. Never mind, forget work! I'm going home to pack a bag now and I'll be right there." I could practically hear him throwing clothes into his suitcase already.

"Tate, just listen to me for a minute. There's no need for that. I'm not alone." I knew that would get his attention.

"Not alone? You're always alone, unless I'm there. Who's with you?" I heard the curiosity in my best friend's voice.

"My neighbor…." I hesitated.

I didn't know exactly how to tell Tate that another man planned to spend the night in my apartment. I was pretty certain that statement would go over like a lead balloon.

"Which neighbor? We don't know any of your neighbors." He stated the obvious.

"Well, I do now. He helped me chase the intruder away, and he's going to stay here in case the psychopath comes back." I recited the words quickly. I knew exactly what Tate's reaction would be.

"*He* is? A *man* who is a stranger plans to spend the night in your apartment, and you're okay with that? You expect me to be okay with that? Willow, are you sure that intruder didn't hit you in the head?" Tate roared on the other end of the phone.

"His name is Marcus Tucker, and he's a police officer. It's perfectly safe, Tate. Omelet even gave him the stamp of approval. Don't be such a worrier." I tried to soothe his panic.

"Forgive me for not putting too much stock in the opinion of your cat. Someone has to worry about you, Willow. I'm the only person in your life who takes care of you. It's my job." His voice was steely with determination. I loved him all the more for it.

"Tate, I know you want to take care of me. You've taken care of me since we were kids. If I thought I was in any danger, I would tell you to run right over here. But I'm not. Marcus is a good guy. He's a police officer. This is kind of his thing." I tried to calm Tate's fears, while also reassuring myself that it was the truth. After all, despite my bravado, I'd never spent the night with a strange man in my apartment before. It was a bit unsettling for me too.

"I guess I have no choice but to trust your judgment on this, but if he so much as touches you…," Tate threatened.

I thought of the way I'd imagined Marcus touching me, and my face turned red. Tate would be furious, and I should be ashamed of myself.

"I'll talk to you after I get home from work tomorrow. I love you." I hoped I hadn't made him angry.

"I love you too, Willow. You know exactly what I mean when I say that." Tate's voice grew serious.

"I do know what you mean," I replied quietly.

"Have you thought any more about it?" Tate questioned.

"Of course I've thought about it, nearly every second for the past week. I think about it all the time. But… I really just don't have an answer right now."

"I know. I'm sorry, babe. That's the last thing you need to be worried about tonight. Just get some rest, and if anything happens, I'll be there in ten minutes."

"You know I'll call you if I need you. I always do. Bye, Tate." I hung up the phone and glanced at Marcus, whose obvious curiosity was written all over his face.

"Boyfriend?" Marcus arched one eyebrow.

"Tate and I have been best friends since we were kids. He's pretty much my only friend, actually." I wanted to explain our complex relationship, but I honestly didn't understand it myself these days.

I had no idea what I wanted from Tate. Part of me longed

for things to stay the way they'd always been. He knew me better than anyone else in the world, and he was in love with me. Moving into a romantic relationship with him would be easy in so many ways. When he kissed me, after baring his soul to me, it took me by surprise. But I had to admit that the kiss had been pretty darn amazing.

Who knew what might have happened between Tate and me if I hadn't stopped him? That leg cramp had been a sign. There was a little voice inside my head warning me that falling in love with Tate had the potential to be disastrous. Until I was sure how I felt, we couldn't go there.

Now, it seemed that life had thrown a wrench into things in the form of a very handsome man named Marcus, who made my heart beat fast and my insides feel like soup. I had a feeling that spending time with him was going to make things more than interesting, to say the very least.

"Your friend seemed upset about me being here. I hope I didn't cause any trouble for you," Marcus observed. "It sounded like he might be a little jealous about having another man here."

"Oh... well, there's probably some truth to that," I admitted.

"If he's just your best friend, he wouldn't be jealous. So, I'm guessing there's a bit more to it than that, at least on his side." Marcus seemed pretty astute.

I went into the living room and began making a bed on the sofa for my new bodyguard. He'd known me only a couple of hours, but he'd hit the nail right on the head. There *was* something more between me and Tate, but I couldn't quite bring myself to put a name to it yet. Too much was at stake to risk making the wrong choice, so I opted to make no choice. It was the coward's way out, but it was the best I could do.

"I really do appreciate you watching out for me, Marcus. Especially considering that until a couple of hours ago we didn't even know each other. And to think, you've already seen me naked," I blurted.

Marcus laughed; he probably had no idea how to respond to my gaucheness. Although it surely wasn't his intention, the wonderful sound of his laughter sent shivers down my spine.

"I'm sorry. I tend to be a bit socially awkward. You'll get used to it." I finished making the bed, and then turned to face my houseguest. "I guess I should try and get some sleep. I have to get up early for work tomorrow. Speaking of which, what are you going to do while I'm working?"

"I told you, I'm your watch. Where you go, I go. Just think of me as a friend who gets to hang out with you all the time." Marcus's words and the thought of spending every waking moment with him made my entire body tingle. *I was in major trouble!* "You have no idea what you've gotten yourself into." I rolled my eyes. "All right then, I guess I'll go to bed now. I hope you're not too uncomfortable on my couch." Suddenly, I wasn't sure I wanted to be in the other room, which seemed so far away from Marcus's protection. All things considered, I was still pretty shaken up. I didn't want to be alone.

I'd always been proud of the fact that I was self-sufficient.

I was not needy, and I'd always had very little tolerance for women who were. That night though, I had to admit that my confidence was shaken. Feminist ideals aside, I reluctantly agreed that having Marcus there to watch out for me felt good.

"Good night, Marcus Tucker, and thanks again for saving my life," I said.

"It was my pleasure. Sweet dreams." Marcus flopped onto the couch, laced his hands behind his head, and exhaled slowly.

I felt his intense brown eyes follow me as I headed to my bedroom. I climbed into bed and stared into the darkness. As physically and emotionally exhausted as I was, I knew that sleep would not come easily. How was I supposed to rest when a man like that was sleeping on my couch?

Chapter Seven

Sleep finally came, and when it did, it came hard. When my alarm buzzed at five o'clock the next morning, all I really wanted to do was toss it out of my floor-to-ceiling window. Anyone who knew me would attest to the fact that I was not a morning person. Unfortunately, my chosen career path forced me into it. If I wanted to make a living, I had to be up before dawn.

"Good morning, Willow." Marcus's deep voice startled me. "I hope you slept well."

I rubbed my sleepy eyes and sighed when I saw his perfectly muscled body leaning on my bedroom doorframe. He was dressed in nothing but his boxers and a T-shirt, causing my pulse to quicken and my throat to go dry. *Breathe, Willow. Don't lose your mind.*

Not used to having to speak to people first thing in the

morning, I tried hard not to be my usual grumpy self. I wasn't fit to be around other humans until after I'd been awake for at least an hour and had two cups of coffee in me. Right off the bat I realized that Marcus was one of those irritatingly perky morning people, but I supposed it was good to discover that there was at least one annoying quality about him. Other than that, he seemed completely perfect.

Dressing quickly, I got myself ready for the day. I decided that I was going to leave Omelet at home, since it would already be awkward having Marcus with me all day. When I explained the situation to her, I could tell she was fine with it. She'd had a busy night and was happy to stay at home and sleep all day.

We stopped by Marcus's apartment on our way out of the building so he could change his clothes, although I thought he looked pretty fabulous just the way he was. He moved quickly, and before long we were headed into Simpson Coffee for our morning caffeine infusion.

"Morning, Willow," Suzanne called as I walked inside. Marcus followed closely behind me, and the confusion registered on her face when she realized we were coming in together. "Hey, Marcus. Are you two with each other?"

"No," I replied quickly, not wanting her to get the wrong idea about us.

"Yes," Marcus said at the same time. Suzanne looked baffled.

"Is it yes or is it no? Do you want an easier question?" she joked.

"Yes, we came in together, but no, we're not… together…

like… well… together," I explained horribly.

"Makes perfect sense to me." She grinned. "The usual for both of you?"

"Yes," Marcus and I answered in unison.

"No Omelet today?" Suzanne asked as she started our drinks.

"She's having a lazy day at home," I replied quickly.

We thanked Suzanne for our coffee and hopped on the bus, arriving at the Dancing Crêpe right on time. The idea of Marcus hanging out with me all day made me nervous. It wasn't that I didn't want to spend time with him. Quite the opposite, in fact. I enjoyed his company immensely. The truth was that I was afraid I wouldn't be able to concentrate on my work with him close by, and my food truck was so small that closeness was inevitable. I would probably be burning crêpes left and right.

I unlocked the door and we both went inside. I gave him the grand tour, which lasted about thirty seconds, since the entire place was just over two hundred square feet.

"This is a nice place you have here. You must be proud of yourself." Marcus leaned on the counter and smiled at me.

"Uh, yeah, it's pretty great. Cooking is all I ever wanted to do." I swallowed hard. The intensity of his smile seemed to always catch me off guard.

"The ballet-themed crêpes are pretty inventive. No wonder they're a hit in Portland. I predict you'll be as big as Voodoo Doughnut one day," he declared.

"That's certainly the plan. I'll be right back." I needed

to finish opening up the food truck. I reminded myself to stay focused on my work, and not on the fact that I couldn't stop thinking about what it would be like to kiss his perfect mouth.

I stepped outside to unlock the housing around my propane tank and was surprised to find it already wide open. That was puzzling; it was unlike me to forget to lock it, but I supposed mistakes happened to everyone, right? Sighing, I reached inside the housing and twisted the valve on the propane tank. It hissed slightly as the pressure inside released.

I went back inside and lit the pilot light on my griddle. I turned the knob and heard the flame ignite. I noticed a slight odor, but didn't think much of it. While I waited for the burner to heat, I gave Marcus a crash course on crêpe preparation. I was a pretty good teacher, and I discovered that he was a quick study.

"If you ever get tired of being a policeman, I think you could have a second career as a crêpe maker. You just might have missed your calling." I smiled up at him and laughed at the look of deep concentration on his face. He was trying very hard not to mess up the batter.

"Don't distract me. This is hard work." Marcus laughed.

"You're a good one to talk about distractions. You've done nothing but distract me since yesterday." My face turned pink as I realized that once again I'd said the words in my head out loud. *There you go again, Willow. You're always sticking your foot in your mouth. Just keep it shut!*

Marcus didn't acknowledge my faux pas, and we worked

side by side for the next few minutes, laughing and talking the entire time. The conversation was easy, and I found myself completely relaxing and enjoying his company. I guess I was worried for no reason about spending the day with him.

All at once, I started to feel lightheaded as the strange aroma grew stronger. It wafted into my nostrils, stinging and pungent. I grabbed the counter to steady myself as the room began to spin.

"I… umm… my head…," I stammered.

Marcus put his hand on my arm, and the look on his face told me immediately that something was very wrong.

"Do you smell something?" I looked at Marcus for an answer, but instead of saying anything, he grabbed me, picked me up in his arms, and dove out the door of the Dancing Crêpe.

We hit the ground rolling, and my body thudded against Marcus's as he took the brunt of the impact. In spite of the fact that he made a perfectly delightful cushion, my body jarred as we landed. I bounced off him and rolled onto the ground, where my shirt became tangled into some nearby wires. I tried to dislodge it, but it wouldn't come loose. Marcus jumped to his feet quickly and dragged me onto mine, ripping my shirt in the process.

I looked around in confusion, still unsure of what was going on. Marcus plucked me into his arms once again and cradled me like a child as he ran at top speed away from the Dancing Crêpe.

"Get out of your trucks. Run! Everybody run! Don't take

anything. Just get out!" As Marcus ran, he yelled loudly at everyone in the nearby food trucks to run as well. I noticed that Katya wasn't in her truck yet, but Hoang was. He took off behind us.

In a matter of seconds, there was a frantic mob scurrying down the busy Portland street. Cars slammed on their brakes, tires screeched, horns honked, and drivers yelled obscenities as the confused, terrified herd of food truck owners and bystanders completely halted the flow of traffic. Once we were on the other side of the street, Marcus placed me on the ground and turned to look behind us.

"Marcus, what's wrong with you? What do you think you're—" I heard a thunderous, earth-shattering boom, and I watched in horror as the Dancing Crêpe went up in flames.

I gasped, covering my mouth to keep the screams from escaping. I couldn't believe what I was seeing. It wasn't possible, was it? My dreams were going up in smoke, literally, right before my eyes. I felt like I'd been punched in the gut. Everything I had worked for would be gone in a matter of seconds.

Why? Why? Why? I didn't understand why any of this was happening. I dropped to my knees, painfully aware of how close to death I'd just come once again. Hugging my arms around my body tightly, I tried to stop my pounding heart and slow my ragged breathing.

"Willow, are you okay?" Marcus knelt beside me and cupped my face in his hands. "Are you hurt?"

"I... I don't think so. I think I'm all right. Did everyone get away?" I was still confused about what was going on, but I was even more terrified that someone may have been injured by my mysteriously exploding food truck.

"Most of the other trucks were empty, but the folks who were there followed along when they saw us running. I'm pretty sure everyone got away in time." Marcus spoke calmly as he took his phone out of his pocket and dialed 911. He finished giving the location details to the dispatcher and hung up the phone. He crouched down next to me again and was just about to say something when a strange expression came over his face. He was looking at something across the street.

I followed his gaze and immediately realized what had caught his attention. A bone-chilling fear gripped my insides. On the other side of the street was a giant of a man—one I would recognize anywhere, even though I had never seen his face. His body shape and demeanor would be forever etched into my brain. My eyes met his and I sucked in my breath. It was the man who'd broken into my apartment last night.

"Marcus, it's him," I whispered.

"I know. I see him too. Whatever you do, do not move. Stay where you are." Marcus flagged down a police officer, who had just arrived on the scene, and instructed him to stay with me. Without another word, Marcus sprinted across the chaotic street. I followed with my eyes, but remained crouched on the ground, too stunned to do anything except follow his directions.

When my attacker saw Marcus coming, he took off, but the giant's hulking body was no match for Marcus's speed and agility. I watched in amazement as he heroically leaped through the air, plowed into the man, and dropped him like a bag of bricks onto the pavement below. There was a scuffle as each man got in his fair share of punches. I winced as the man swung his meaty fist and connected with Marcus's face, causing his head to snap back. But Marcus wasn't deterred. He kicked the assailant in the stomach and dropped him to his knees.

Without hesitation, he pulled the attacker's hands behind his back and whipped out a pair of handcuffs. My heart beat wildly as I watched the unbelievable scene unfold on the other side of the street. When the man was securely detained, Marcus dragged him roughly to his feet and led him back to me. My mouth was agape at what I'd just witnessed.

"Since I saw his face myself yesterday, I already know the answer to this question, but I'll ask anyway. Is this the man who attacked you, Willow?" Marcus asked as he tried to catch his breath from the scuffle.

I nodded; the words wouldn't come.

"Who hired you? I know you aren't smart enough to pull this off on your own," Marcus barked at my attacker. "You broke into her house last night. I saw you with my own eyes. And I'm guessing you're the one who just tried to blow us all up. What did you do, puncture the line to the propane tank?"

The man glared at me. "You might want to watch your back. She is really out to get you."

I would never forget the sound of his voice; I shivered in fear.

Realization that this man had tried to end my life, not once, but twice within twenty-four hours was enough to nauseate me. This was a serious situation. Someone wanted me dead, and whoever it was seemed to be pretty insistent upon making it happen quickly. I was in trouble, deeper trouble than I'd ever been in before. And that was saying something for me. This even beat the time that I was held hostage by a bank robber. At least in that case, I was just an innocent bystander, not an obvious target. I always seemed to be in the wrong place at the wrong time.

About that time, an ambulance, four more police cars, and three fire trucks arrived. *Fire trucks.* That meant Tate would be arriving soon. Once he realized the location of the fire, he would be in a panicked, mad rush to find me and be sure I was still alive. I really should have called him to let him know I was fine, but I knew he was on one of those trucks and probably wouldn't answer.

I decided a text would be better than a call. He worried about me more than anyone else in my life. Now that he fancied himself in love with me, that protectiveness would be even more intense. I pulled my phone out of my pocket and sent the message.

Willow: Just want you to know that I'm okay. The Dancing Crêpe is history, but I'm all in one piece. Call me as soon as you can. I love you.

I knew he wouldn't see it before he arrived to fight the fire, but I knew I'd be getting a call from him as soon as he could make one. Marcus led my attacker to the back of one of the nearby police cars and he was hauled away to the station.

He might be gone for the moment, but I knew this ordeal wasn't over by a long shot.

The wheels in my head were turning. Who could want me dead that badly? I didn't think I had any real enemies. I was practically a social pariah; I really just did my best to avoid everyone. I was kind, but kept to myself for the most part. I was a fair business owner, and I didn't cheat people. I was a pretty stand-up citizen, if I did say so myself. To the best of my knowledge, I hadn't given anyone any motive to kill me. As far as I could tell, everyone liked me well enough.

I kept trying to piece the puzzle together. Then suddenly, like a bolt of lightning, a possibility introduced itself. It forced me to retract my earlier statement—not everyone liked me, and I certainly didn't like everyone. In fact, there was one person I disliked intensely. *Elizabeth.* I didn't like her, and she surely didn't like me, but I didn't hate her enough to kill her. Even though I joked about it, I would never actually consider doing it. When Officer Peterson had asked if anyone might want to hurt me, should I have told him about Elizabeth?

It was hard to say. The fact of the matter was this—I was the only thing standing between her and the entirety of my father's billions. At least that was my assumption, unless a prenuptial agreement existed. Other than me and Elizabeth, there was no one to inherit his money. If that wasn't motive to get rid of me, then I didn't know what was. The thought was sobering. I'd always known that woman was bad news.

"Keep a lid on your crazy thoughts, Willow," I whispered

to myself. "You can't go throwing around attempted murder accusations without any proof."

Yes, proof was something I needed before I could even entertain that idea. If I were wrong, I would do far more damage than even I could imagine. But one thing was certain; I needed to keep a close eye on my wicked stepmother. *Keep your friends close and your enemies closer.* That's exactly what I intended to do.

I watched in stunned silence as the firemen worked to put out the flames. I searched for Tate, but it was hard to tell which one was him under all of the fire gear. Hopefully he'd already received my text, although I knew that was a long shot. With nothing left but smoke and ashes, the stark reality of what happened was hard to ignore. Everything I had worked so hard for was obliterated.

My business was gone, and if it weren't for Marcus's quick action, my life would have been too. Everything in the Dancing Crêpe was destroyed in the all-consuming fire, and it looked like several of the other food trucks had sustained some major damage as well. I wondered if destroying everything had been the plan, or if it had been a bigger explosion than the killer had intended. It started in my food truck, so I was obviously the target. Sadly, the villain's vendetta against me had hurt the businesses of those around me as well. I kept reminding myself that I was lucky to be alive and no one else had been hurt. It was all I could do.

My food truck could be replaced, and because of my insurance policy, I knew it would be. Still, it all felt like a complete defeat to me. It would take some time to see it as anything else. Fortunately, time was something I had.

I gathered my wits about me and rose to my feet. All I could do was keep putting one foot in front of the other. I walked slowly to where Marcus stood talking with another police officer. His back was to me, but the other officer's eyes practically bulged out of his head as I approached. He stared at me, mouth gaping open, while I tried to figure out what he was looking at. It didn't take me long to understand.

Glancing down, I realized with horror that my shirt was torn right down the middle, and the remaining pieces did little to cover what was underneath. *Again? I always seemed to be naked these days.* About that time, Marcus turned to see what his fellow officer was gawking at and then scolded him for staring. He walked over to me and blocked me with his body.

I could tell Marcus was attempting to make me smile when he said quietly, "Ma'am, you are going to have to learn to keep your clothes on, or I'm going to have to arrest you for indecent exposure. That's twice in twenty-four hours that you've lost them."

Knowing that if I didn't laugh I would end up crying, I replied, "I'll keep that in mind. Just be sure you know what you're asking for."

Marcus took off his sweater and wrapped it around me. "You are just an accident waiting to happen, aren't you?"

"I've been told that a time or two. You know, you've managed to save my life twice in less than one day. Not too bad. You're very good at your job," I congratulated him.

"It's a life worth saving, I think." He traced the tip of his finger over my cheek and wiped a streak of dirt away. I shivered, partly because my clothes had melted off me, and partly because being that close to him did something strange to my insides.

"What do I do now?" Everything in my life was in complete disarray, and I had no idea what came next.

"Well, first of all, we need to go to the police station. We're both going to have to give our statements. It shouldn't take long. After that, I think you should go home and rest. I doubt you'll be getting a lot of work done today." Marcus looked sadly in the direction of what used to be the Dancing Crêpe.

"But I don't want to go to the police station. What if they ask me to pick him out of a lineup or something? I don't ever want to see that man again." I sighed.

"If they ask you to do it, then you need to do it, Willow. You have to do whatever you can to get that man off the streets. You'll be able to see him, but he won't be able to see you. Don't worry," Marcus soothed.

"Someone is trying to kill me. How can I not worry?" At the moment, I couldn't imagine ever feeling secure again.

"I'm going to take care of you. I promise." Marcus sounded so sure, and I wanted to believe him, but I was terrified.

"Okay, I'll do it. Are you coming back to my house with me when we're done?" I realized that I was hopeful that the answer was yes.

"Of course. I told you, I'm your security detail until

we're sure you're safe. At this point, you're in even more danger than before. I'm going to push to be assigned to you until this is over. You're stuck with me."

"Stuck with you… I think I'm getting the better end of that deal," I replied.

"Don't be so sure of that," he countered. "I find you to be more entertaining than anyone I've ever met. Not to mention that I have to really be on my toes to hang out with you. It's good for me."

I felt my phone vibrate in my pocket and pulled it out to read the text from Tate.

Tate: Got your message. I'm coming to your house as soon as I can get away.

Willow: I have to go to the police station to give a statement, but I should be home before long.

Tate: I'm going to give you the biggest hug of your life when I see you.

Willow: I'm counting on it.

Tate: You're going to give me a heart attack from worrying about you. I love you, babe.

Willow: Love you too.

Chapter Eight

Marcus and I had been back at my apartment for a couple of hours when I heard a loud banging on my front door. He instinctively reached for his weapon, but when I heard Tate's frantic voice on the other side, I told my eager bodyguard to take it down a notch. I took a deep breath before opening the door for Tate. Things were about to get ugly.

"Willow, what on earth is going on? I just spent the morning dousing the flames on your exploding food truck. Last night you were attacked in your apartment. This is not normal, even for you. All I could think of was the time I had to pull you out of your car before it burst into flames because you were trying to burn Patchouli incense to make it smell good. I swear you're going to kill me." Tate crushed my body in a bear hug. His strong arms gripped me tightly.

"I… can't… breathe," I managed.

"Sorry, but I've been scared to death ever since I got the call about the fire. No, I take that back. I've been scared to death since you told me you were nearly killed last night." Tate released his grip and stepped away. His eyes were troubled, and I hated the fact that I'd once again stressed him out.

"I'm fine. See… I'm all in one piece." I gestured to my body and smiled, hoping to lighten his mood.

"You're not fine. Someone is trying to kill you, and I—" He stopped abruptly, and I knew he'd spotted Marcus, who was stretched out on my couch looking perfectly at home.

Tate's jaw clenched. I knew that look far too well. He was not at all pleased with my houseguest. I was sure he'd imagined Marcus as a grizzled, grumpy old policeman, not the fine specimen of a man that he was in reality. I could smell his jealousy from a mile away.

Marcus yawned and lazily pulled himself up to a sitting position. He cracked his neck, rotated his shoulders, and rose slowly to his feet. His calm, relaxed demeanor was the opposite of Tate's anxious, amped-up state of mind. I wondered if Marcus was purposely trying to get under Tate's skin by showing how comfortable he was in my home, or if he was really as laid-back as he seemed.

He sauntered across my living room and stood beside me. "You must be Willow's old friend, Tate. I'm Marcus. It's nice to meet you."

The two men stared at each other for several seconds. Neither spoke; neither moved. It was a standoff. It was two male wolves, each trying to establish himself as the alpha dog. The tension in the room was so thick it could have been cut with a knife. It was ridiculous, but I had to admit it was a little flattering too. I had two gorgeous men, each puffing himself up and trying to impress me. That wasn't something that happened to a girl every day, at least not this girl.

"Tate, Marcus. Marcus, Tate. Now that we're all friends, can you both stop sizing each other up, please? It's making me uncomfortable." I cleared my throat. "Let's go into the kitchen and I'll make us a snack."

Feeding people was what I did best. It was my answer to everything. I figured the guys could get to know each other while I made lunch. Once they were better acquainted, everything would be fine, right? Even as the thought entered my brain, I knew it wasn't likely. Tate and Marcus were both strong men, and right now both of them saw me as the damsel in distress, which made them feel the need to be my rescuer. *Typical guys.*

Tate was obviously jealous, since he was in love with me. Strangely, though, I got the feeling that Marcus was a little jealous of Tate as well. *Why would that be? Is Marcus interested in me?* We'd definitely shared a couple of moments, and I'd thought of kissing him more than once. Perhaps the feelings were mutual.

Marcus and Tate sat down across from each other at my kitchen table. Tate's fists were clenched. He bounced his legs up and down quickly, obviously agitated. I learned a long time ago that my best friend was laid-back and easygoing about everything—except when it came to me. It was even worse now that he was romantically inclined toward me.

Marcus, on the other hand, sat casually in his chair; he

was the picture of relaxation. True, I'd only known him for one day, but I had the distinct impression that he was always like that. He was confident, in charge, not easily ruffled, and he didn't seem to question the fact that he would always get exactly what he wanted. The two men couldn't have been more different, and I realized that I was drawn to both of them, each for entirely different reasons. That was not good. In fact, it was very bad.

Why does my life have to be so complicated? That was exactly the reason I avoided people. I should not be trusted around other human beings. Sighing, I prepared grilled cheese and pastrami sandwiches on sourdough and pretended to ignore the heated conversation happening between the two men at my kitchen table.

"There's no reason for you to be here anymore. I'll stay with Willow, so you can go back to wherever it is you came from." Tate cut straight to the point.

"That's not going to happen. I told her I would watch her, and I'm not going anywhere. In case you haven't heard, someone broke into her apartment and tried to kill her. That same person tried to blow her up inside her food truck today. She needs me, and I'm not leaving," Marcus replied.

"You're a cop, right? Weren't you with her when the Dancing Crêpe exploded this morning? It doesn't seem to me that you're doing her much good by being around. It's not like you were able to stop it from happening." The anger in Tate's voice was palpable.

"No, I didn't stop it from happening, but I did get her out in time, and she wasn't hurt. It seems to me that you should just go stick your fire hose into someone else's business. Willow doesn't need it here," Marcus sneered.

"Wait just a minute, you—" Tate slammed his clenched fists onto my table. The wilting flower arrangement in the center vibrated from the force.

"Hold it right there. Both of you shut up!" I yelled at them as I pivoted quickly away from the stove.

Both men froze. Their eyes widened in shock at my outburst. I was a little surprised myself. I didn't normally yell at people, but I wasn't sure how else to stop the obvious competition between the two men.

"You need to listen, and listen well. Tate, you are my oldest and dearest friend. I love you, and you know it. There's nothing to prove here. Marcus, I just met you, but you've managed to save my life twice, which I obviously appreciate very much. It seems to me that I need both of you. So you're just going to have to suck it up and find a way to get along. End of story." I placed both hands on my hips and tried to look intimidating. I was sure it didn't work.

"Sorry, Willow." Tate hung his head in contrition.

"Yeah, sorry, I guess I got carried away," Marcus agreed.

"Yeah. Whatever. Can we all just move on now? Lunch is ready." I rolled my eyes and served the grilled cheese, hoping food would help everything.

Both men devoured the sandwiches. It appeared that neither of them had eaten in months. When he was finished, Tate stood up, gathered everyone's dishes, and carried them to the sink where he proceeded to rinse them. It wasn't unusual. Tate always did the dishes and cleaned the kitchen when I cooked. It was our unspoken agreement. Marcus, however, watched with a look of defeat on his face. He was obviously keeping score, and Tate's tidying of my kitchen had just earned him a point in the competition.

"Since you're not alone right now, I'm going to run next door and grab some more clothes. I also need to check in with my sergeant and see if they've approved my request to be assigned to you. It looks like you and I are probably going to be roommates for a while, so I'll need to bring some more of my things." Marcus smiled, and his gaze darted toward Tate, whose shoulders stiffened visibly as he was loading the dishwasher. It wasn't hard to detect the smugness in Marcus's voice. The dynamic between the two men was really very interesting, and I might have even found it comical if it weren't so irritating.

"Go on, Marcus. Tate and I will be just fine. Take your time," I replied.

Tate had finished the dishes, so I grabbed his hand and led him into the living room, where we both flopped down onto my couch.

"Oh, I won't be long. Try not to miss me too much." Marcus smirked at Tate and then grabbed his apartment key and headed out the front door.

"What a jerk," Tate mumbled under his breath.

"He's not a jerk. He's saved my life twice. Be nice," I warned.

"I've been crazy thinking about something happening to you, Willow." Tate scooted across the couch and took my hands into his. The worry on his face was almost more than

I could stand. I hated the fact that he was upset.

"But nothing *did* happen, Tate. At least nothing that can't eventually be fixed. I'm fine, thanks to Marcus." My eyes met his and I had to look away. The depth of feeling I saw there scared me more than a little bit.

"Willow…." Tate cupped my face in his hands.

Everything about him was so familiar to me. No one knew me better than he did. So, when he leaned in toward me and pulled my body close to his, it seemed perfectly natural to let him. He was my best friend. I loved him. *But in what way?*

His lips met mine, soft and gentle, and I responded. I couldn't help it; I wanted to. Being with Tate was like being home. There were no pretenses. It was just real. I threaded my fingers through his thick blond hair and took the kiss deeper. It was so good, being with him like that. It was even better than I remembered from the last time we tried it. He was familiar and soothing to me. It was exactly what I needed at that moment.

I had no idea what I was doing. I was kissing Tate again, and I'd been thinking of kissing Marcus since last night. *Don't be an idiot, Willow. You are going to get in way over your head, just like always. Do the smart thing for once and keep your distance from both of them. This is why you don't do relationships, remember? Because you're not mature enough to handle it.* I pulled away from Tate.

"Why did you stop? You know we're right for each other, Willow. You feel it. I know you do. You should stop trying to fight it. No one else can even come close to the history we have with each other." Tate smoothed my hair away from my face.

"I love you so much. And I'm attracted to you. I'll admit it. You're gorgeous and sexy, and I'd have to be blind not to be. But I'm not sure it's the same way you feel about me, and until I am sure, we need to cool it. You're my best friend, and I would rather cut my own arm off than ruin that. I'm confused, and I don't know what I want. And I know I'm giving you mixed signals by continuing to kiss you, but I like kissing you. Please be patient with me." I sighed heavily.

"I'll be patient. But I can't help the way I feel about you. And I can't promise I won't kiss you again." Tate grinned deviously, and I laughed. He always knew just what to say.

"Well, honestly, I can't guarantee that I won't kiss you back." My heart was racing in my chest. Tate's eyes drew me in deeper. "As a matter of fact, I want to kiss you again right now." I leaned in and touched my lips to Tate's at the exact moment the front door opened and Marcus walked in. I jumped as I heard the door close. Tate smiled, looking like the proverbial cat that ate the canary.

"I hope I'm not interrupting anything. Where should I put my stuff, Willow? I'm sure you don't want it scattered all over your living room." Marcus raised an eyebrow in question.

"Um… you can put it… in… my bedroom." I could feel Tate's eyes on me.

"Sounds good to me. Your bedroom it is." Marcus winked at me and carried his bags into my room.

"Your bedroom? He's sleeping in your bedroom?" Tate jumped up from the couch.

"I haven't worked through all of the arrangements yet, Tate." I sighed.

"Why doesn't he go sleep in his own apartment? I'll stay here with you." Tate pulled me to my feet.

"Marcus is the professional in this area, Tate. He's watching me—like a bodyguard. He says he should stay here until we find out who's trying to kill me."

"A bodyguard? You've seen that movie, right? You know what happens? She falls in love with the bodyguard! I don't like it. I don't like it one bit." Tate clenched and unclenched his jaw.

"I know you don't. And I don't like knowing that Marcus's presence is necessary to keep me alive because someone wants me dead. But that's just the way it is." I placed my hand on his arm to soften the blow.

"There has to be some other way—" Tate's words were cut short by the sound of his phone beeping. "Ugh, I have to go. I volunteered to cover a shift at the station if they needed me. I'll check in with you tonight."

Marcus came back into the living room just as Tate was hugging me goodbye. I felt his body tense up in my arms when he saw his rival.

"See you later, Tate. Don't worry about Willow. I'm sticking to her like glue. She's safe with me." Marcus smiled, and I knew for sure that he was trying to get under Tate's skin.

"She better be, or you'll have to answer to me," Tate

threatened, slamming the front door as he left. That all went about as well as I'd anticipated.

"He seems like a nice guy." Marcus's voice was practically dripping with sarcasm.

"He is. He's one of the nicest guys I know, as a matter of fact. He's taken care of me my whole life, Marcus, and he's not used to having someone else around. Cut him some slack, all right?" I suddenly felt very defensive of Tate. I was on an emotional roller coaster.

"Hey, I'm sorry. I was just messing with him. I'll do better next time, I promise. I don't want to upset you." Marcus gently placed his hand on my arm to soothe me.

My heart pounded inside of my chest. I could still taste Tate's kiss on my lips, so why was I imagining what kissing Marcus would feel like? I'd gone from no romantic interests to two of them in less than a day. Between that and the fact that someone was trying to kill me, I was exhausted.

"I think I'm going to go lie down for a while. I'm sure you can entertain yourself out here while I'm gone, right?" I backed away from Marcus, suddenly needing to put some space between us.

"I can entertain myself out here. Unless you want me to come and sit next to you, you know, for safety." The spark in Marcus's brown eyes turned my insides to mush.

"As tempting as that sounds, and believe me, it sounds tempting, I think I just need some time alone." I backed even farther away from him before I could change my mind and agree.

"How about this? You go lie down and I'll make you

some hot tea. I'll bring it to you when it's done." Marcus was pulling out all the stops.

"That sounds like an excuse for you to weasel your way into my bedroom."

"Nah, I think you're right. You need to rest." Marcus headed into my kitchen and turned on the kettle.

"Okay. See you in a few minutes." I retreated into the bedroom.

Marcus was using some kind of reverse psychology on me. I was the one who said I wanted to be alone, but now that I was alone, I sort of wanted him to be with me. I was a screwed-up mess.

I climbed into my bed. Looking at the bandage on my arm, I realized that it would need to be changed soon. Maybe Marcus would help me with it. I remembered how tender his hands were when he tended to my wound last night, and I felt a rush of warmth.

Sighing, I sank all the way down until I was wrapped in the covers up to my chin. I wanted to sleep, but the thoughts in my head were churning. I thought of Tate and Marcus, and the fact that neither of them was going anywhere anytime soon, and I had no idea what I was going to do about that.

I'd always been the girl who avoided relationships, telling myself that none of it was real anyway. I didn't need the headache, and I liked being alone. Alone was good. Alone meant that I didn't get hurt, and I couldn't hurt anyone else.

But then Tate had told me he loved me, and I started to think about things that I'd never before considered. I'd actually tried to picture what a relationship with Tate might look like—right down to the white picket fence and the children. That picture had made me smile. I saw us as an old couple, rocking side by side on our front porch as I complained and he tried to make me laugh. A future with Tate didn't seem so horrible, if it worked out as it was supposed to. Unfortunately, I'd also seen the picture of what could happen if it didn't. I saw me and my crazy, paranoid, cynical ways slowly deteriorating Tate and his beautiful optimism. I saw me destroying everything we had with each other, and that picture terrified me.

He'd put up with my eccentricities since we were kids, he made me laugh, he protected me, and best of all, he knew how to put me in my place when I needed it. We made a great team—as best friends. *So why would I want to go and potentially ruin that?* Getting involved with Tate in a romantic way would be a disaster, because I was a mess. Tate would be perfect, and I would destroy him. I just had to remind myself of that the next time I decided I wanted to kiss him. I needed him as my best friend, and since there was no way to guarantee a successful romantic relationship, it was out of the question.

And then there was Marcus. He'd certainly come out of nowhere and completely blindsided me. How was it possible that I could be so attracted to someone I'd just recently met? I knew nothing about him, other than the fact that he was a cop and he was dangerously sexy. My intuition told me that he was also a genuinely good guy, which only added to the allure of the total package. I had the distinct feeling that he was equally attracted to me, and I had no doubt that if I kissed him, he'd kiss me right back. It was all just one big, fat problem. To top it all off, someone also wanted me dead very badly.

I closed my eyes and tried not to think of the biggest problem at hand—being the target of a murderer. My happy little love triangle paled in comparison to that issue. I'd tried telling myself that I should just not think about it, but that was ridiculous. My mind was consumed, replaying every single detail of my near-death experiences. It was difficult to understand that some woman in my life wanted me dead so badly that she had hired a hit man.

Try as I might to find other options, I kept coming back to Elizabeth. As far as I was concerned, she was the only one who hated me enough to want me gone. The fact that she would benefit from my death seemed logical. As Dad's third, very young wife, the only way she was going to get her hands on any real money someday was if I wasn't around to inherit it. I had always been the sole beneficiary of my father's wealth. It had never been an issue with any of his other wives, because there were always prenuptial agreements in place. That might also be the case with Elizabeth, but something told me it wasn't. She had my father wrapped around her little finger in a way that none of my prior stepmothers had. As long as I stood in between her and the billions, I was a threat to her happiness.

Other than being a selfish, gold-digging bimbo, she had lived a pretty clean life as far as I knew. I didn't think she had any real skeletons in her closet, and I wasn't aware of her having any kind of checkered past. I couldn't just accuse someone like Elizabeth of murder without some concrete proof.

I suddenly remembered the slip of paper that the investigating officer found on my living room floor with the phone number written on it. Something about the number was familiar, which was exactly the reason I'd memorized it.

I grabbed my cell phone from the nightstand. Scrolling through my contacts quickly, I went all the way to the W's—for wicked stepmother, of course. I blinked twice to be sure I wasn't imagining things, but there it was.

I gulped. The phone number I'd memorized from the slip of paper found at the crime scene—my living room—belonged to Elizabeth!

Was that proof? In my mind it was, but the professionals would probably say that finding my own stepmother's phone number lying on the floor of my apartment didn't mean anything. The more I thought about it, the more I realized that maybe I was just being paranoid. I would have to keep looking until I found something else. Or maybe I should just tell Marcus about it.

"Knock, knock." I heard Marcus's voice outside the bedroom door.

"Come in," I called.

"I come bearing gifts." Marcus placed a tray on the nightstand. He'd brought me tea and cookies, both arranged beautifully on one of my best plates. He knew the way to my heart was through my stomach, and he was pulling out all the stops.

"Wow, that looks lovely, Marcus. Thank you." I smiled up at him, suddenly self-conscious, although I had no idea why.

His smile made me want to swoon. I probably would have, if I were the swooning type. "I aim to please, ma'am."

"Yes, well you're doing a good job of it," I replied.

He didn't say anything else. He just stood there looking at me, and all I could do was gaze back at him. He completely unnerved me.

"Umm… can I ask you something?" I began nervously.

"Sure, ask me anything," he replied.

"If I found something that might be… evidence… I should tell you, right?"

"Evidence of what?"

"From the attack."

"Yes, of course you should tell me. You should tell me right away. What evidence do you have?"

"Remember that slip of paper that was on my floor? The one with the phone number on it?" I was very worried about bringing it up, but I knew I had to.

"I remember. What about it?"

"Well, I knew the number looked familiar, but I couldn't place it at the time. So I memorized it. I just now looked in my contacts, and the phone number belongs to…." I hesitated.

"It belongs to Elizabeth Simpson. I assume you're related," Marcus finished.

"You know about the number? How do you know?" I was shocked!

"It was taken as evidence, and Officer Peterson called the number right away. When we found out it belonged to someone with the last name of Simpson, we realized that the intruder probably didn't drop it. I mean, it was a family member's phone number found in your house. It's definitely not proof of anything."

"Elizabeth is my stepmother. Why didn't you tell me they called it?" I asked.

"Because it wasn't important. The officer didn't seem to think it meant anything and neither did I," he replied.

"Yeah, that's what I thought too," I lied. It might not be proof to the cops, but to me, it was enough. The police didn't know how much Elizabeth hated me, or how much she stood to gain by getting rid of me. But I knew. "You know, Elizabeth and I don't get along very well…."

"That's a pretty common thing with stepmothers, I imagine," he smiled.

"Yeah, I suppose so. I mean, it probably doesn't mean anything that we practically hate each other." I didn't want to accuse her, but I also didn't want them to completely rule her out.

"Hate is a pretty strong word. Do you think she would harm you?"

"No, I don't think so…." Now that I'd brought it up, I was chickening out. I didn't want to believe she could hurt me, but I couldn't think of anyone else who would either.

"So, your relationship is fairly normal?"

"Define normal," I sighed.

"Willow, do you believe that your stepmother wants

you dead?"

Yes! Yes! Yes! The word played over and over again in my head, but I couldn't bring myself to say it. "No, that would be crazy, right?" I shook my head and tried to dismiss the thought.

"Well then, I'm going to go flop on your couch and watch some TV for a bit. Enjoy your quiet time." Marcus bent down and tipped my face upwards.

He moved toward me slowly and my tummy turned, anticipating the feeling of his lips on mine. *He's going to kiss me!* I closed my eyes and felt the slight brush of his mouth. I was just about to pull him closer when he stopped, stood up, and exited the bedroom without another word.

He left me reeling, trying to figure out what had just happened. *Is he playing hard to get with me? Did he just kiss me, or did I imagine it?* My mind raced with thoughts of what might have happened if he hadn't stopped. I had to admit that I'd wanted nothing more than to pull him close and kiss him again. Luckily one of us had some self-control.

Chapter Nine

That evening, Marcus and I lounged in my living room as darkness settled in all around us. The only light in the room was the hazy glow of the television. I was fetchingly decked out in my fanciest yoga pants and the one T-shirt I found in my drawer that wasn't completely holey. Most women would have pulled out the sexy lingerie or at least a pretty nightgown with a man like Marcus spending the night in her apartment. I wasn't anything like most women.

Marcus may as well get to know the real me, the unglamorous me. I was the type of girl who didn't give a hoot what other people thought. As attracted as I was to him, I knew I couldn't be anything other than my authentic self. Even if I'd wanted to pull out all the stops, I honestly had no idea how to even try to be sexy. That was so far out of my wheelhouse that it wasn't even funny. Marcus and

I would both find out soon enough if he actually liked the person I was. Either way, I wasn't big on pretenses, and I certainly wasn't going to change that for a man—no matter how gorgeous he was.

Marcus had changed into plaid boxers and a blue T-shirt boasting the word Police. We sat on opposite ends of my couch, watching the ten o'clock news while I tried not to doze off. I was sure there would be something on during the broadcast about the fire at Cartlandia, and I wanted to stay awake long enough to see if the investigation had turned up any new information.

To an onlooker, Marcus and I probably appeared to be a typical couple hanging out together before bed. The only things out of the ordinary were the gun and Taser staring ominously at me from my coffee table. Seeing them lying there made me more than a little bit anxious. I couldn't believe these objects were necessary to keep me alive, but apparently they were.

Earlier, I had told Marcus they made me uncomfortable, but he gently reminded me that his job was to keep me safe, and he intended to do that in whatever way was necessary. I knew he was trained to use both items safely and professionally, so I tried to calm the warning voices in my head.

I watched intently as the anchor person behind the news desk told the story of the suspected arson case involving the Dancing Crêpe. It was horrific to watch the replay of the clip of firemen dousing the flames incinerating my precious food truck. Seeing it again made it hit home even more. A part of me kept hoping that I would wake up to discover that none of this was real. But that wasn't to be. I was watching it right before my eyes on the news.

It wasn't a nightmare, but an unfortunate reality, and there was no new information on the case, according to the annoyingly perky anchorwoman. I thought she should have at least pretended that the story disturbed her. *How could she smile when she was talking about my food truck exploding?* When she finished the report, I grabbed the remote and turned off the television. I'd had enough of her, and more than enough of the day. I was ready for bed.

"I'll bet that was tough to watch, wasn't it?" Marcus scooted closer to me on the couch.

"It's all just so unreal." I rubbed my temples as my head started to ache.

"You know, it would be perfectly normal for you to yell, or cry, or... something." Marcus put his arm around my shoulders and I shivered. "You've been pretty emotionless all day, and I get the feeling that's unlike you."

"I'm sure it'll come, Marcus, and knowing me, it will come at the absolute worst moment. It will come out of nowhere. That's how I process things. Right now, I just feel numb," I confided.

"Don't hold it in. I hope you feel comfortable with me. I realize that your life has been turned completely upside down. You have a virtual stranger sleeping in your apartment, and you are being hunted by a murderer. You need to talk about it, and I'm a great listener. I should be, since I grew up with five sisters." Marcus planted a quick kiss on the top of my head.

"Wow, five sisters? No wonder you're such a great guy. You know, I'm really tired. We should go to bed. I have to deal with insurance stuff tomorrow, and I have a feeling that's going to make for a long day." I started to stand up from the couch, but then realized that we hadn't yet discussed sleeping arrangements. *This is going to be interesting.*

"When you say 'we should go to bed,' what exactly do you mean by that?" Marcus looked unsure for the first time since I'd met him.

"Well…." I chewed nervously on my lip, trying to come up with a good answer.

I wished I could request an easier question. "I'll be the first to admit that my couch isn't designed for sleeping. I mean, it's comfortable and all, but it's not a bed, and you are here to take care of me. You were already stuck on the couch last night. I would feel extremely selfish if I slept in the bed again and you were out here. So, maybe you should take the bed and I'll take the couch." It seemed like a perfectly logical plan to me. It was definitely the safest idea.

"Absolutely not, Willow. I will not take your bed away from you. First of all, you need your rest. Second of all, the couch is between the front door and your bedroom, which is exactly where I need to be."

"Don't be ridiculous. You're not going to get any rest on my couch," I argued.

"I'm here to protect you, not to rest," he insisted.

"How can you protect me if you're sleep deprived?

Besides, you're not here in an official capacity. You're here on your own time, doing this crazy thing out of the goodness of your heart. At least you can have a good night's sleep."

"Well, you're not sleeping on the couch. End of discussion." He was certainly a stubborn man.

It was completely exasperating that I couldn't come up with a better choice. It shouldn't be this difficult a decision. "Oh, what's the big deal, anyway? Let's both just sleep in the bed. We're adults, right? It won't be a problem. Besides, then you'll be right next to me if you need to turn into Super Cop."

"Sleeping in your bed certainly won't be a problem for me." Marcus leaned toward me and brushed a light kiss across my lips. *That came out of nowhere!*

Now why did he have to go and do that? Wanting to resist, but knowing how weak I was, I responded hungrily, even as I scolded myself for doing so. That man had me in the palm of his hand, and I felt helpless to fight the magnetism. So I did the exact opposite. I threw my arms around his neck and pulled his face closer to mine, kissing him fiercely.

Marcus whispered in my ear as we came up for air, "I think you've bewitched me." He attempted to gain his composure a bit before he continued, "That was unprofessional. This is definitely not the way I usually guard people."

The sound of his voice snapped me back to reality. There was some kind of magic going on here, but it seemed to me that I was the one who was under a spell. I wasn't acting like myself at all, and I needed to start immediately before it was too late.

"I'm pretty sure it's the other way around." I cleared my throat and put some space between our bodies. Marcus took my hand, pulled me to my feet, and led me into my bedroom.

Although I knew this could very well lead us into the exact territory I was trying to avoid, I followed willingly. We both sat down on the edge of my bed, and I tried to steady my breathing. *Get a hold of yourself, Willow.* Unfortunately, I knew my ability to do so was virtually nonexistent. I was the equivalent of a weak, out of control, hormonal teenager where Marcus was concerned.

I sighed as his face moved closer to mine. *Here we go again.* When our lips met, my resolve to take things slowly began to crumble, piece by piece. With the last shred of coherent thought, I pulled myself away again. "We need to stop."

Marcus, whose body remained close to mine, pulled his face away enough to ask, "The rational part of my brain agrees with you. The other part wants to know why we need to stop. Is it such a bad thing that we're attracted to each other?"

"No, it's not bad. Unfortunately, it's quite good. But you don't understand. This isn't me. I don't do relationships, at all—not ever. And there's Tate. I don't know what's going on with us." I nervously twirled my hair around my finger. I hated all this talk about emotions. It made me uncomfortable and squirmy.

"You know what's funny? I don't do relationships either. I swore off them entirely a couple of years ago. I got burned pretty badly by a woman I cared about deeply. I was very much in love with her, and then I found out she wasn't who she pretended to be. Since then, I haven't met a girl I liked enough to waste my time with. Until yesterday, that is." Marcus smiled and his dimple showed. That dimple was going to be the death of me.

"You mean when I barged into your house naked, bleeding, and hysterical? I was pretty hard to resist." I rolled my eyes, embarrassed.

"Yeah, actually, I mean exactly that. It's going to sound stupid, and I'm probably losing my advantage by being honest with you, but I knew as soon as I saw you that you weren't just any ordinary girl. You're mouthy and opinionated, you're strange as can be, and I never know what you'll say next. You're annoying as all get out, and nothing at all like the kind of girl I usually go after. But oddly enough, I like it. All of it. Like I said, you've bewitched me." Marcus traced my cheek with his finger.

"Well, the feeling is pretty mutual, if you need to know the truth. That's what scares me. I'm not sure what it means that I'm this attracted to someone I barely know. Throw in my confusing feelings about Tate, and the whole situation seems like a recipe for disaster." My eyes met his and I held his gaze.

"You're the chef. Maybe you just need to tweak the recipe." Marcus's voice was like a caress.

"Yeah, maybe I do. I've got a lot to figure out, Marcus. I don't want to hurt you or Tate, but I know that hurting one of you is inevitable. Besides, we only met yesterday, for goodness' sake! Just give me some time," I replied quietly.

"Take all the time you need. I'm not going anywhere." Marcus raised my hand to his lips and kissed it softly. It was the exact same thing that Tate said after I kissed him.

Then he stood, pulled me to my feet, and hugged me. It was so intimate, somehow even more so than kissing him. I liked how safe I felt in his arms, but the biggest part of me was just confused and scared by all of it. I certainly had a lot of things to figure out.

Before I knew what was happening, Marcus pulled the covers down on my bed and turned around and scooped me up into his arms. I gasped as my feet left the ground. He was full of surprises. He bent and gently placed me on the bed. Not at all sure what he was doing, I smiled when he pulled the blankets up to my chin before tucking them tightly around my body.

"Are you tucking me in?" I giggled.

"I am. I offer full-service body guarding, including nightly tuck-ins." He chuckled as he walked around the bed and eased himself under the covers on the other side.

Somehow, he had managed to place the gun and Taser on the bedside table without me even realizing he'd done so. He was good. I felt safe. We both snuggled under the blankets, trying to get comfortable for the night. The situation was strange and complicated, but what was even crazier was the fact that I didn't feel uncomfortable with him lying in bed next to me.

"You know, I've never been tucked into bed before." My voice was quiet in the darkness, and even though I tried to hide it, I'm sure Marcus detected the sadness behind my words.

"C'mon, that can't be true. Didn't your mom ever tuck you in?" Marcus asked.

"She might have. I don't really remember. She died when I was five." Tears gathered in my eyes, and I willed myself not to let them fall. *I am not going to cry again!*

"I'm sorry. I didn't know about your mom. What about your father? I'm sure he tucked you in at least a few times, right?" I listened for pity in his voice, but I didn't hear it. There was only compassion, and that was the impetus I needed to open up a bit more.

"He never tucked me in, not once. He wasn't that kind of father. He couldn't even stand the sight of me when I was young. He said I reminded him too much of my mother." It was a truth I'd never spoken to another human being besides Tate.

"That's a lot for a little kid to handle. It sounds like you've had your fair share of sadness. No wonder you try to avoid relationships," Marcus replied.

"Yeah, well, it's okay. You don't need to hear my sob stories." I cleared my throat, angry at myself for revealing so much to him.

Things were easier when I just ignored my feelings. It became far too complicated if I allowed myself to trust another person, so I had to try very hard not to let him inside. Trust made you vulnerable; just look at what was happening with Tate.

One of us would get hurt if I let him in, and more than

likely it would be me. I needed to find a way to put up my familiar wall, but with Marcus it didn't seem to work. He was able to see everything I was trying so hard to hide.

"I want to hear all of your stories, the good ones and the bad ones. I know we don't know each other that well yet, but don't be afraid to talk to me. I promise I won't let you down." He squeezed my hand.

"Talking about my feelings isn't really my thing. I think I'm just stressed out with everything that's happened. I'm not going to cry again, so if you're waiting for it, don't hold your breath." I tried to force some spunk into my voice, but it just sounded hollow and empty to my ears.

"We'll see about that. I'm determined to get beneath that sassy facade you put up to hide the real you. I'm going to figure you out, just wait and see. You have trust issues, but someday I want to know you the way Tate does. Good night, Willow." He squeezed my hand one more time before he released it and rolled over in bed, turning his back to me.

Omelet jumped into bed and curled up in a ball on the pillow next to my head. Her soft purring helped to soothe me. As I lay in the stillness, I thought about what it would feel like to have Marcus know me that well, and to know him in return. It was scary and exciting at the same time.

Up to that point in my life, Tate was the only person I'd ever really let inside of my wall. He was the only one I trusted enough to be there. It had taken him a lifetime to gain that trust, and I wondered whether or not I could ever feel that comfortable with someone else. I closed my eyes and begged the strange, uncomfortable, unfamiliar thoughts to just go away.

Chapter Ten

When I awoke the next morning, I was surprised to see the light already filtering in through my bedroom windows. Waking up to brightness in my bedroom confused me. I couldn't remember the last time my alarm hadn't gone off before dawn. Then everything came crashing back into my brain, and I remembered that I hadn't needed to set my alarm last night. I no longer had a reason to get up early.

I grabbed my phone off my bedside table and blinked twice when I saw that it read ten o'clock. How was that possible? When was the last time I'd slept past five? Owning a crêpe truck required early mornings, but after yesterday's explosion, I didn't own a crêpe truck anymore. The thought was like a fresh punch in the gut.

Glancing at the bed beside me, I noticed that Marcus was no longer there, and much to my chagrin, I realized

I was afraid. Someone had tried to kill me twice already, and I was sure he would succeed the next time. What if the giant-man were in my apartment again? What if he were in the other room, waiting to do the deed? *He's in jail. He can't hurt you.*

My breath came hard and fast, and my heart raced inside my chest as I tried to calm myself. Every creak in my empty bedroom sounded exponentially louder than usual. I wanted to get out of bed, but I was paralyzed by a deep sense of fear.

Something crashed inside my bathroom. I sat up in bed, clutched my pillow to my chest, and let out a bloodcurdling scream. In a flash, Marcus was at my side, pulling me close inside his protective arms.

"What's wrong? What happened?" he asked.

"I woke up and you were gone. Then I heard a creaking sound and I thought the intruder was here. Then something crashed in the bathroom and I couldn't even move. All I could do was scream," I babbled. By that time, I was sobbing and gulping for air. Although I knew I was being irrational, I couldn't seem to get a handle on my fear.

"Hey, I told you I wasn't going anywhere. I was just out in the kitchen. Willow, you're okay. Look at me." He angled my face toward his and forced me to focus on his eyes. I felt my heartbeat begin to slow, and my breathing returned to normal. "I'm not going to let anyone hurt you." He smoothed my hair and rubbed his hand up and down my back in comforting strokes.

"But I heard something in the bathroom." I knew I'd

heard a crash. "I might be scared, but I'm not crazy."

About that time, Omelet trotted nonchalantly out of my bathroom, took one look at her blubbering mess of a human, and exited the bedroom.

"Must have been the cat?" Marcus asked, and I nodded, feeling like a complete idiot.

How had I gone from a competent, self-sufficient woman to a foolish girl afraid of her own shadow in only a couple of days? I wanted the old Willow back, the girl who was sassy and feisty and wasn't afraid of anything. But I didn't know how to make that happen. That girl seemed light-years away. Frustrated, I did the only thing I seemed capable of doing—I cried again. Good old Marcus just kept holding me. I was sure he thought I was turning into a one-trick pony.

"Do you think maybe this was the breakdown you were referring to last night? The one you said would come out of nowhere? I think maybe you're starting to process all of those pesky feelings," Marcus suggested gently.

"Probably." I nodded and gulped for air, trying to calm my ragged breathing. "You can just say it. I'm a mess." I unceremoniously wiped a trail of snot on the sleeve of my T-shirt.

"You're not a mess. You have every right to break down. It's healthy and completely normal," Marcus soothed.

"Embarrassing, that's what it is." I pouted.

"After what we've been through together, you're embarrassed by a few tears? Now that is crazy." He laughed.

"Jerk." I punched him playfully in the arm.

"I have an idea. Why don't you go clean the snot off yourself, and I'll take you somewhere fun. Go on." Marcus rose from the bed and pulled me to my feet.

"Where are we going?"

"To a place where all of your problems will just melt away," Marcus hinted.

"Give me another hint," I requested.

"It's the most delicious place in Portland, besides The Dancing Crêpe, of course," he prompted.

"You don't mean… Voodoo Doughnut?" I asked excitedly.

"Is there anywhere else?" He laughed at my obvious elation.

"All right, I'll be ready in ten minutes."

It was surprising that he knew exactly what to do to make me feel better. He'd figured out pretty quickly that I was a junk food kind of girl. He'd known me only a couple of days, but I was discovering that he had keen intuition. Whatever, I wasn't going to argue with him if it meant that a trip to Voodoo Doughnut was in my immediate future.

I moved at lightning speed and was ready to go in just eight minutes, congratulating myself on being two whole minutes ahead of schedule. After the week I was having, some delicious, sugary, fluffy doughnuts were just what the doctor ordered, and I couldn't get my hands on them soon enough.

Marcus and I threw on our rain jackets—this was Portland after all; if it wasn't raining right then, it would be before long. Omelet had curled up on her bed for a cat nap, so I whispered in her ear that I would bring her a treat when we returned, and then we walked a block to the nearest bus stop.

Usually during my ride, I popped in my earbuds and ignored the other riders, but that day was different. In spite of the fact that I was excited to be heading out with Marcus, I was trying to be a million times more vigilant than usual.

My eyes darted back and forth between the passengers sharing my space. Normally I was the sort of girl who went through life minding her own business, but that morning I decided to look closely at each stranger. What if the person trying to kill me was on this bus? What if she'd been following me through my days and I hadn't even noticed? I had to admit that I wasn't exactly observant. I might have been sharing oxygen with a murderer and didn't even know it.

As I glanced at each face, I didn't see the giant-man who attacked me. He would have stood out like a sore thumb, after all. As far as I knew, he was locked up at the local police station where he belonged. At least I hoped so. In a perfect world, he wouldn't be seeing the light of day anytime soon.

My thoughts continued to wander. Even if the hit man were in jail, I also had to worry about the person who had hired him. Some woman wanted me dead, and she'd paid him a sum of money to try to make her wish come true. Even worse, he'd said she was someone I knew. She might be following me around every day while I existed in a state of complete oblivion. I shivered at the idea. It was all too creepy. Marcus, who was squeezed on the seat next to me, glanced my way.

"You okay?" His forehead creased with obvious concern.

"Sure. I'm great. Why wouldn't I be?" I forced a smile.

"Well, forgive me for not stating the obvious, Willow."

"I'm fine. Sorry about that breakdown this morning. I've got a handle on things now. It won't happen again." I forced bravado I didn't feel.

"You should let yourself break down."

"Nah, I have to keep my crazy in check. Freaking out is totally unnecessary, and not on the agenda. Case closed." I managed to put some steel into my voice.

Marcus could probably see right through my lies, but I didn't care. I needed to find the girl who wasn't afraid of anything; if I looked hard enough, I knew she was still in there, somewhere. *I hope so anyway.*

The bus pulled up to our stop, and we squeezed through the sea of people and exited. Marcus grabbed my hand protectively. We crossed the street and headed toward the pink building with the brightly colored sign festively adorned with the store's iconic voodoo doll shape. The line wrapped all the way around the block, but in true Portlander fashion, Marcus and I jumped right into it without even batting an eyelash.

Rain or shine, there was always a line at Voodoo Doughnut. The line didn't even matter; it was really just part of the whole experience. There weren't many places where I would happily stand and wait that long for anything, but I didn't even think twice about it. It was worth every second spent for a taste of the gourmet, doughy goodness. Truly, there weren't many things in this world as delicious as a Voodoo Bacon Maple Bar.

Marcus and I chatted while we stood in the queue, and I furtively scanned the crowd for anyone who might appear the least bit suspicious. I had to keep my eyes open for whoever was after me. She was determined, so I needed to be on my toes. I knew Marcus was there to protect me, but I had to help him out. I would do whatever I could to make sure I stayed alive. Never mind the fact that I had no idea who I was looking for.

I was getting in touch with my surroundings when I heard Marcus gasp loudly and swear under his breath. Glancing at him, I knew immediately that something was wrong. His face looked pained and angry at the same time. I was just about to ask him what the problem was when I spotted a problem of my own heading right for us.

"Willow Simpson, I haven't seen you since we almost had lunch together. You're looking… messy… as always." The high-pitched, overdramatic, aristocratic voice of Cinnamon St. James assaulted my eardrums. I would know that voice anywhere. I had despised it since elementary school. My hands curled involuntarily into fists, and I stuffed them into the pockets of my rain jacket.

"Cinnamon… I wish I could say it was good to see you, but it's not." My spine stiffened rigidly as it always did when I saw her.

"You two… uh… know each other?" Marcus stammered.

"Unfortunately. Do you know her?" I demanded of him

as I pointed to her.

"Are you two, like, together?" Cinnamon flipped her waist-length pale blonde hair and glared at Marcus and me with her perfectly shaped blue eyes. I hated her for being so beautiful. I always had.

"Wait a minute. Marcus, you obviously know her," I said.

"Well," he started.

"We know each other pretty well, as a matter of fact." Cinnamon batted her spidery lashes. I wanted to punch her so badly. I knew it would feel just as wonderful as I'd always imagined.

"Where did you two meet?" Marcus asked me, obviously uncomfortable.

"We went to school together. I've had the unfortunate experience of knowing Cinnamon since we were kids. To make matters worse, she's my stepmother's best friend." The thought was nearly too much for me to stomach. "Now it's your turn, Marcus. How do you know her?"

"Cinnamon and I… we… uh… well…," Marcus sputtered.

"Marcus and I were engaged," Cinnamon replied triumphantly.

"You… were engaged to… her? Did you fall and hit your head? Were you declared temporarily insane?" I couldn't believe Marcus had been engaged to Psycho Barbie.

He'd told me he'd sworn off relationships after a broken engagement. He'd said he'd loved the woman very much. Was this who he was talking about? It wasn't possible.

How on earth could Marcus have loved a horrible person like Cinnamon? If that was the kind of woman he went after, how in the world could he be attracted to me? Was I the comic relief?

"You're certainly slumming these days, Marcus. I thought you were supposed to replace up, not down." Cinnamon glared at me.

"Statements like that are exactly why we're no longer together. You have no regard for other people's feelings. How dare you say something like that about another human being?" Marcus retorted.

"You don't need to defend me," I explained to Marcus. "I've despised her since the first day I met her. She's a waste of oxygen."

"Willow! I can't believe you said that," Marcus exclaimed.

I learned long ago that the best way to handle Cinnamon was to resist giving her the reaction she was looking for. She wanted to get under my skin, so I tried not to let her know that she had. Glancing in front of me, I was relieved that the line had moved to the point that we were almost inside the front door.

"Well, it's obvious to me what Marcus sees in you, Willow. I mean, you are the sole heiress to the largest fortune in Portland. At least you were until Elizabeth came into the picture. No man could possibly want you for anything besides your father's money." Cinnamon's smug statement cut more deeply than I cared to admit. It took every ounce of willpower for me to resist knocking her perfect teeth out.

"Cinnamon, Willow, that's enough!" Marcus barked.

I moved closer to my rival until my eyes were almost level with hers. I stood so close that our noses practically touched, and I continued taunting her. "I actually feel sorry for her, Marcus. She's always wanted what she couldn't have. She never got over the fact that the one person she pined away for wouldn't give her the time of day. She hated that Tate was so loyal to me. It was really quite sad to see how she threw herself at him. Apparently, seeing the two of us together has just reminded her of yet another thing she doesn't have. Looks like I got both the men you wanted, doesn't it, Cinnamon?" I winked, and then laughed in her face before stepping away.

"You little—" Cinnamon began.

"See you around." I grabbed Marcus's hand, and we stepped inside the building, leaving her fuming on the sidewalk.

I breathed a sigh of relief that the confrontation was over. As much as I tried to pretend that she didn't bother me, girls like Cinnamon St. James always had. I couldn't stand the fact that I felt inferior to her perfection, and yet I did. She was smart, athletic, popular, and she'd done everything she could to make me feel horrible about myself since we were kids. She made fun of my red hair, ridiculed me for my freckles, and berated me for my lack of style and grace.

"Are you okay? You two certainly went at each other. You're obviously not friends. I'm sorry we ran into her." Marcus put his arm around my shoulders.

"Why are you apologizing? You didn't do anything

wrong, other than be dumb enough to get yourself engaged to a woman like that. Besides, I'm used to her." It irritated me that she was the woman Marcus had been involved with, the one he'd loved.

"So, let me get this straight. Your dad is married to Elizabeth? I met her a few times, and she's certainly a piece of work. That must have been awkward for your dad to marry someone your age," Marcus replied.

"Well, technically Cinnamon and Elizabeth are two years older than I am, but basically, yes. My stepmother is someone I grew up with and went to school with. I told you before that I have a lot of baggage," I replied.

"Yeah, I'm beginning to see that." He nodded.

"You and Cinnamon, huh? I'd have never imagined you with a woman like her. I mean, obviously she's beautiful. There's no denying that. I would have pegged you as a guy who was after a little more substance though. Guess I was wrong." I wasn't sure why it bothered me so much that Cinnamon was Marcus's ex-fiancée, but it did. It bothered me a lot. Mostly it made me wonder what interest he could have in a girl like me if she was the kind of person he was attracted to.

"I guess I was blind to what she was really like. I fell in love with her, and I fell hard. I think she was good at pretending to be what I wanted, but she couldn't keep that up forever. Eventually I started to see past her exterior and realized that I wasn't as much in love with the inside. Plus, I think she finally figured out that she would never be happy as a cop's wife. It's not a very glamorous thing at all, and I didn't run in the same social circles as her family and friends. It was a mismatch from the start. I was pretty broken up about it for a long time though." I heard the pain in his voice, and it angered me that Cinnamon had hurt him.

"You won't be surprised to hear that I think you're way better off without the likes of her. If I never saw her or my snake of a stepmother again, it would be too soon."

Marcus and I reached the front counter and placed our orders. It was always such a dilemma to decide which doughnuts to buy; they were all equally delicious. After the agonizing decision, the euphoria of excitement set in. I couldn't wait to devour them. With our pink box in hand, we headed back to my apartment.

We chatted while we rode the elevator up to our floor. I couldn't wait to get started on my Portland Cream doughnut. I was imagining the first bite and was practically salivating in anticipation. Not a moment too soon, the elevator doors slid open and we walked down the hallway toward my apartment.

I was surprised to find a pink Voodoo Doughnut box already sitting on the floor in front of my door. I looked up at Marcus and noticed that his jaw was set. He didn't look happy at all. Obviously I wasn't the only one who found it odd.

"Don't touch it. Let me." Marcus bent down and slowly approached the pink, square box. He opened the lid.

Inside the box was a voodoo doll doughnut whose raspberry filling was leaking out as if it had been stabbed too deeply by its pretzel stake. The bottom of the box was thick with raspberry, and it looked like the voodoo doll was swimming in its own blood. Across the top of the inside of the box, finger-painted in red jelly, were the words *WATCH YOUR BACK.*

Now I was angry. It was one thing to try to kill me, but to suck the joy out of a box from Voodoo Doughnut was really crossing the line. It was unforgivable. The person who had done this was a monster.

It was obvious to me that the box came from Cinnamon. It was too much of a coincidence to believe anything else. She'd been furious with me when we left her on the sidewalk earlier.

But then I realized that she probably had no idea where I lived, unless Elizabeth had told her. It would have been pretty hard for her to beat us back here with the box too. If it wasn't her, then was it Elizabeth? The hit man?

"This just further cements the fact that I can't leave your side." Marcus picked up the box and carried it inside my apartment, where he promptly placed it into a plastic bag and sealed it tightly. Apparently it was evidence.

"It might be from Cinnamon. She was jealous to see us together. Maybe this is her snide little message to me."

"I'm pretty sure it's not her. This honestly doesn't seem like something she would do. I mean, come on, can you imagine her smearing jelly all over that box? It would mess up her manicure or get on her designer clothes. Something like this isn't her style at all." Marcus plopped down at my kitchen table and opened our box of doughnuts. He took a huge bite of his Grape Ape.

"Well, if not Cinnamon, then who? The hit man? Isn't he locked up?" I sat down across the table from Marcus and licked the chocolate frosting off my Portland Cream.

"Actually, he's not. His lawyer got him out on a technicality. There wasn't enough evidence to hold him." Marcus spoke quietly.

"You knew he wasn't in jail?" I dropped the doughnut on the plate in front of me. I suddenly had no appetite. "Why didn't you tell me sooner?"

"I didn't want you to freak out, like you're doing right now. I'm not going to let him hurt you, Willow."

"Why didn't they lock him up? Why wasn't there enough evidence?" I couldn't believe this was happening.

"His lawyer is good. I don't know how a thug like that is able to afford a hotshot lawyer, but somehow he did." Marcus took a deep breath and continued, "Here are the facts: the man broke into your apartment, but he had a mask on so they argued that you couldn't actually identify him. His lawyer said that he was too far away from me when I chased after him for me to have possibly been able to see his face clearly. There was no other evidence besides the two of us saying it was him. It's all circumstantial. So he's out, for now. I'm going to get him though. I promise you." Marcus stuffed the remainder of his doughnut into his mouth and slowly licked the frosting from his fingers. Watching him distracted me from my problems for a minute. Then the minute passed.

"I can't believe that guy is freely walking the streets. That's not okay with me. He tried to kill me twice! Doesn't anyone care about that?"

"I care, and he won't get within an inch of you again."

I couldn't believe this was happening to me. That man was going to kill me, and no one except Marcus was doing anything about it. I knew it with every fiber of my being. I wasn't safe, no matter how much my volunteer bodyguard assured me otherwise.

I was dizzy, and my breathing felt strange. I needed oxygen. Someone had sucked all the air out of the room. I could feel all of my rational thoughts slipping away, and hysteria came creeping in.

I'd only been this upset a couple of times in my life, and Tate had always been the one who could talk me down from the ledge. Suddenly, I knew I needed him. I dug through my purse frantically, looking for my phone. My hands trembled and my eyes blurred with the tears that were now flowing freely down my face.

"What are you looking for, Willow?" I heard Marcus's gentle voice somewhere in the back of my mind.

"Tate. I need Tate." I kept searching in my purse, but I couldn't seem to find my phone.

"I'm here. I'll keep you safe," Marcus assured me.

"I need Tate. Now!" I demanded as I continued to search frantically.

"Okay. I'll find him." Marcus took my purse out of my hands, reached inside, and pulled out my phone. He scrolled through my contacts until he found the right one.

"It's Marcus. Can you come over, please? Willow needs you." He spoke softly, but I heard the sadness in his voice loud and clear. I didn't want to hurt him, but at that moment, he couldn't give me what I wanted. I needed Tate's familiarity. Nothing else would do.

Marcus hung up the phone, took my hand, and led me into the living room. I sank into my couch, and he sat down next to me.

"Tate will be here soon. He just got home from work. Everything is going to be all right." He grabbed my hand in his, and I noticed that it felt icy cold inside his warm one.

I nodded my head as the tears continued to fall. Tate would be there soon, but deep in my gut I knew that nothing would be all right as long as the person who was trying to kill me walked the streets.

Chapter Eleven

Just twenty minutes later I heard a key in my front door before it burst open and Tate strode in. I jumped from the couch and ran into his arms, hurling myself at him like a battering ram against an iron gate.

"Babe, it's okay. I'm here now. Everything is going to be just fine." Tate whispered soothing words that only I could hear while he caressed my back.

I buried my face into his chest and sobbed. I was terrified; it seemed as if nothing would ever be fine again, despite the fact that everyone kept saying so. But as he had since we were kids, he held me and told me to let it all out, so I did. He was the only person with whom I'd ever felt completely comfortable being myself. I didn't need to fake happiness or bravery with Tate. Besides, even if I'd tried, he would have seen right through it. I knew I was safe to be my messed-up self with him, and that's exactly what I did at that moment. It felt like my life was spiraling out of control.

"We're going to get through this together, Willow, just like we've done everything else in our lives. Come sit with me." Tate grabbed my hand and led me to the couch, where Marcus was already seated. Situated between both men, I slowly began to calm down.

I wondered what Marcus must have thought as he watched Tate and me. I'd been trying to put on a brave front for him, but I just couldn't do it anymore now that I knew my attacker was wandering the streets of Portland a free man. I was terrified, and no amount of sassy, brave attitude on my part could conceal that anymore. I needed Tate to keep me grounded. I knew I needed Marcus too, on a professional level anyhow. I couldn't think about him as anything more than that at the moment.

"What happened? What triggered this?" Tate directed his questions to Marcus, who shifted in his seat and looked a bit uncomfortable under my best friend's scrutiny.

"She's upset over the attack and her food truck, obviously. We just took a little outing, and there was a not-so-pleasant surprise in front of her door when we returned." Marcus's voice sounded defensive, and I felt sorry for him. Tate, when he was in protective mode, was a force to be reckoned with.

"Cut the crap, Tucker. She was fine when I left her with you yesterday. She was upset, but fine. Now she's a puddle of tears, and she was practically hyperventilating when I got here. I want to know what happened! You're supposed to be taking care of her!" Tate roared.

"It's not his fault, Tate," I said quietly. "Marcus is just the bearer of bad news. He told me that the man who attacked me is not in jail. They didn't keep him."

"Didn't keep him? How is that even possible? You both saw him! That's two eyewitnesses!" Tate's voice raised another octave.

"Technically, Willow didn't see him. His face was covered with a mask. When I chased after him, I saw his face, but the jerk's hotshot attorney argued that I couldn't possibly have identified him properly from that far away. There wasn't enough evidence. They let him go." Marcus leaned forward on the couch and rested his face in his hands. I knew he wasn't any happier about this than I was.

"Unbelievable. He tries to kill her twice and the cops just tell him to go home? Go have a nice life? How is that justice?" Tate exhaled loudly and slumped on the couch.

"It's not justice. But I can assure you that I will not rest until I find that man and he's behind bars. I can promise you that." Marcus's voice was like hardened steel.

"Well, that's probably the first thing you've said since I met you that doesn't make me want to punch you in the throat," Tate answered, and the two men glared at each other.

"What do we do now?" I asked quietly.

"We do the same thing we've been doing, Willow. Your attacker might be free, but he won't get close to you as long as I'm around. And I can promise you that I'm not going anywhere," Marcus responded. "But I do have some more bad news, I'm afraid. I got a call from the precinct, and since they let the guy go, they're not going to pay for a security detail for you."

"So what happens to me? Today is your last day off. You'll have to go back to work tomorrow." I hadn't wanted him there to begin with, but after everything that had happened, I was afraid to be alone.

"I'm still trying to come up with a solution. I have some sick leave stored up. If it comes to that, I'll use it," Marcus replied.

"You're not using your sick time for me. I won't have it," I insisted.

"I'm not going anywhere either. Marcus might be the cop, but you need me for moral support. I'll be staying here too when I'm not at work," my best friend concluded.

"That's not necessary, Tate. I know you want to be here for me, but—"

"It's *not* up for debate, and I *will* be staying with you until further notice." He left no room for questions.

"Well now, won't that be cozy? Where are we all going to sleep? I'm not sharing a bed with you too, Randall," Marcus said with an eye roll.

"Me too? What does he mean by that, Willow?" Tate jumped off the couch. "Did you sleep with him?"

"Yes, we slept together, but we only *slept*. Nothing happened." I tried to calm him down, but the look on his face told me that I was epically failing.

"I wouldn't say that *nothing* happened exactly. At least it felt like something to me." Marcus looked pointedly at me, and I could tell I'd hurt his feelings. Things were quickly going from bad to worse.

"Well, maybe it was something, but it wasn't what Tate thinks it was," I argued. The conversation was making me uncomfortable, and I knew I had to defuse the bomb before it exploded in my face. "Let's just drop this, for goodness' sake!"

"Listen," Tate began, but was stopped by the ringing of my phone.

I jumped off the couch, grateful for the interruption. I'd never been so happy to answer a phone before. I grabbed it off the kitchen counter and took a deep breath before pushing the button. I saw on the caller ID that it was my dad, and I had no doubt that he would have a million questions about what had happened to me. We had been playing phone tag for days.

He'd been out of the country on business, and I'd called him and left messages after the attack in my apartment, as well as after the food truck explosion. He'd returned both of my calls, but I'd missed them. He'd left a message saying that he would be calling that night after he arrived back in town, and that I had better answer if I knew what was good for me.

"Hey, Dad," I said as I picked up the phone. "Before you freak out on me, yes, I'm just fine."

"Don't be ridiculous. You are anything but fine, Willow. As soon as I heard what happened, I wanted to head right back home, but I had meetings scheduled in Amsterdam that I couldn't get out of. You know that, right?" Dad's voice sounded concerned, and I had no doubt that he was, but I had been preempted by his business meetings for as long as I could remember. I was used to my position somewhere down the line in terms of importance. It used to hurt, but I'd gotten over that a long time ago. I knew where I stood with him.

"Of course I know that," I lied.

"Well, I'm back now, and I'm taking control of this situation. I'll be hiring a personal bodyguard for you, effective immediately," Dad demanded.

"That's not necessary, Dad. Tate is here right now," I began.

"Tate Randall is a firefighter, not a bodyguard. You need more than him."

"My neighbor, Marcus, is here too. He's been with me since the attack, but he has to go back to work tomorrow. He's a police officer," I explained.

"Put him on the phone. Let me talk to him," Dad commanded.

"You don't need to talk to him. You can talk to me. I'm a grown woman. You don't need to 'handle' me." I rolled my eyes. Some things never changed.

"Willow." My father sighed heavily. He was perpetually frustrated by his inability to control me. "Fine, what do you know about him?"

"He saved me from the attacker, saved my life when my food truck exploded, and hasn't left my side for a second. I'm in good hands. Not to mention the fact that Tate is here, and he plans to follow me around when he's not at work.

Trust me, Dad, I'm being watched by far more people than I want to be." I sighed loudly.

The guys were great, and I really did appreciate the fact that they were taking such good care of me. The truth was that I was a loner, and more than anything, I just wanted some space. A normal woman would be thrilled to be cooped up with two gorgeous men, but I wasn't a normal woman. As much as I wished for it, I knew that alone time wasn't headed my way anytime soon.

"Willow, I don't care if the head of the Secret Service is with you. A man broke into your apartment and tried to kill you. Then your food truck exploded. That same man knows where you live. You said in your voicemail that someone you know hired him. You aren't safe there. You are packing up your things immediately and you and your entourage will come and stay with me." Dad spoke the words as if the whole thing had already been decided.

"Absolutely not! That's not going to happen. I can't live at your house." I took a deep breath and cleared my throat. I couldn't believe I was having this conversation. It was ridiculous. "Dad, I love you, but are you insane? Elizabeth and I can't live under the same roof. We will kill each other, and then you won't have to worry about me being murdered."

My father was crazy if he thought I was going to live with my stepmother, and for more than the obvious reason of our mutual hatred. As far as I was concerned, Elizabeth might be the one who'd hired the would-be assassin in the first place.

Marcus's ears perked up when he heard me mention staying at my father's house. He walked toward me and motioned for me to give him the phone. Confused, I placed it into his hand.

"Mr. Simpson, my name is Marcus Tucker. I'm the police officer who has been staying with your daughter. Yes, I do understand the gravity of the situation, sir. Unfortunately, it's not in the police budget to hire twenty-four-hour protection for Willow. No, I'm just as unhappy about that as you are, sir. I overheard your conversation, and am I correct in assuming that you believe your daughter should stay with you until this case is solved?" Marcus was all business.

I heard him say "Yes, sir," "That's a generous offer, sir," and "I couldn't agree more." When I heard the final, "We will see you soon, Mr. Simpson," I knew I was in trouble.

Marcus agreed with my father, and they were obviously ganging up on me. He hung up the phone and placed it on the counter. I knew what he was going to say before he opened his big mouth.

"Your father just hired me to be your security detail. The amount that he offered is staggering. I just have to clear it with my boss. Looks like I will be using my sick leave after all." Marcus smiled.

"I'm glad you'll be watching me, but he's crazy if he thinks we're going to his house," I insisted.

"Your father is right. I've been trying to come up with a place to take you for the last few days, knowing full well that you're a sitting duck in your apartment. His suggestion is the perfect solution, so you and I will be staying at your father's until further notice," Marcus explained.

"And me. You're not leaving me out of this." Tate joined us in the kitchen.

"Let me think about it for a minute… umm… no, no, and no! You don't understand. I can't live with Elizabeth. I despise her, and she despises me." I paced back and forth in front of the two men, not quite able to believe that I was even having this absurd conversation.

Should I just tell them that I was certain Elizabeth was the one who hired the hit man? That would change their minds for sure. But as enticing as the idea sounded, I couldn't sling around that accusation until I had some proof. I knew I had to keep my mouth shut.

"Be realistic, Willow. Your dad's house has like twenty bedrooms and fifteen bathrooms in it. You can easily avoid Elizabeth if you want to," Tate countered.

Obviously, I knew I could avoid my stepmonster, but given how much I loved to irritate her, I probably wouldn't. It was too hard for me to resist. I sort of enjoyed pushing her buttons. Still, the thought of living under the same roof was torture. I didn't want to do it.

"Elizabeth is annoying and won't be easy to avoid, I'll give you that. But I will be there to help you, and from the sound of things, so will Tate," Marcus said as he glared at my best friend.

"Hmm, it sounds like you already know Elizabeth. How?" Tate asked Marcus curiously.

"It's a long story," Marcus began.

"Actually, it's really not all that long. Marcus here was

engaged to Cinnamon," I blurted out, more than happy to change the subject for a minute.

"You were engaged to Cinnamon St. James? Oh, that is hilarious!" Tate began to laugh, a deep, belly laugh that made the corners of my mouth turn up. I couldn't wait to hear where this conversation was going to go.

"It's not…. I mean, she's not so bad… I just didn't know her as well as I thought I did. It's been a couple of years since we broke things off." Marcus looked uncomfortable and sad, and I felt sorry for him, but I was also dying to know the real story. I had a feeling there was a lot he was leaving out. There was a kind of pain in his eyes when he talked about her, and it made me wonder if he was really over her or not.

"Cinnamon is a snake, or a vulture, or some other kind of horrible animal. She's been trying to get her claws into me since primary school. It's really pretty funny. Every time she sees me, she can't help but throw herself at me." Tate laughed. Marcus shifted his weight and looked a bit angry.

"And Cinnamon hangs out at the house with Elizabeth every single day. Are you sure you still want to move in?" I asked smugly, certain I'd just found the one thing that would convince both Marcus and Tate that moving in to my Dad's house was the worst idea ever.

"Granted, it will be… difficult… seeing her… to say the least." Marcus cleared his throat. "But being at your father's house is the safest thing for you, so that's what we will do."

It was obvious that Marcus's past with Cinnamon wasn't something he liked to talk about, and I couldn't blame him.

Next to Elizabeth, I would be hard pressed to think of a worse person in the whole world.

"It's settled. We're going today," Marcus commanded.

"I guess I have no say in this decision, do I? Whatever. I'll go pack my things," I relented.

"I'll go pack up too and meet you back here in forty-five minutes. We can take my truck." Tate kissed my forehead and whispered, "It's going to be fine," before he left.

"You have no idea what you've just agreed to," I said quietly to Marcus.

"I know exactly what I've agreed to. I've agreed to keep you safe. It's my job, and that's the only thing that matters right now." Marcus brushed his thumb over my cheek, and I shivered.

Chapter Twelve

I continued to drag my feet, and it took much longer than the boys anticipated to get me out of my apartment. I had to do some basic cleaning if I was going to be gone for a while, and I was hungry, so I had to make us all a snack. I took my sweet time packing up my belongings, and then I had to pack for Omelet too. After running out of reasons to delay the inevitable, we finally left at eight o'clock that evening, much to the guys' frustration.

We headed down the road in Tate's immaculately restored red 1966 Chevy truck. My body was jammed in between my two babysitters on the bench seat. Omelet sat on my lap looking confused and angry. She didn't like to be away from home, and she knew that something was wrong. I would be lucky if she ever forgave me for upending her entire life.

Our luggage shifted in the bed of the truck while I tried to convince myself that everything was going to be just fine. Deep down, I knew I was headed straight toward certain disaster. Nothing good could possibly come out of this living arrangement. I was sure of it. Oblivious to my dark mood, Marcus and Tate argued animatedly about football. It seemed they couldn't even agree on that. I just wished for the day to end quickly.

We exited Portland's city limits and headed toward the Southwest Hills. I felt my frustration grow exponentially as we drove past some of the most luxurious, outrageously beautiful homes a person could imagine. I'd grown up in this area, in a house that made even the most brilliant of these mansions look like shacks.

Now, every time I visited my father, I cringed a little bit. As a child, I remembered feeling guilty that we had so much while others had so little. I still felt like that. The way my father flaunted his wealth was an embarrassment. His outrageous wealth had been just one more thing to set me apart from everyone else. Even though my peers' parents were rich, they weren't in the same league as Barringer Simpson. We were the richest of the rich. The Simpson wealth was legendary, so I was an outcast, even within our elite social circles.

We climbed to the top of the hill and arrived at the gargantuan gate situated in the trees. Tate punched in the gate code on the keypad, and it slid open slowly, granting us access to the Simpson estate.

The driveway twisted and turned through the forest for

about a mile. Finally, the house appeared out of nowhere, and I heard Marcus catch his breath when he saw it. It really was quite a spectacle, and most people had the same reaction the first time it came into view.

My father had built the house with sheer wow factor in mind, and it certainly accomplished its desired goal. Designed in the Mediterranean style, the four-story mansion was complete with exterior rendering, characteristic archways, and a red-tiled roof. It really was something to behold, with its various balconies, porticos, and ornamental details. The driveway directly in front of the house boasted multicolored tiles forming a mosaic of a coffee cup with the word Simpson below it.

When Tate said that the house had twenty bedrooms and fifteen bathrooms, he was only exaggerating a little bit. In reality, it had fifteen bedrooms and ten bathrooms, certainly nothing to sneeze at by any means. A person could literally get lost inside the maze of rooms. You practically needed a map to find your way around. As magnificent as it was to look at, it had been a cold and uncomfortable place to grow up.

"Well, here we are. You asked for it." I glared at Marcus, who simply patted my leg and smiled.

"It's beautiful. I can't believe you grew up here," he replied. I could tell he was more than impressed.

"Yes, the mind reels that someone as unpolished as little old me came from all of this, doesn't it?" I asked sarcastically.

"I didn't mean it that way. I just meant that I can't

imagine living in a house this fancy. This is certainly out of my league on a cop's salary." Marcus was practically salivating as he fixed his eyes in wonder on the mansion. It always had that effect on people.

"Yeah, no wonder you and Cinnamon didn't work out, Marcus. You weren't quite up to her expectations and standards. Her parents have almost as much money as Willow's," Tate quipped.

"Come on, you guys, no fighting. This is going to be bad enough without me having to babysit the two of you and break up fights." The three of us scooted out of the truck and grabbed our bags from the back. I clipped Omelet's pink leash onto her rhinestone collar, and she trotted along behind me, looking even angrier than before. She didn't want to be there any more than I did.

"Good evening, Miss Willow. Allow me to take your luggage." George, the English butler I'd known since birth, smiled at me and took the bag out of my hands.

"Hello, George. Looks like you'll have to be putting up with me again. This time I've brought along a companion or two." I stood on my tiptoes and planted a quick kiss on his cheek. He chuckled softly.

"It's not 'putting up' with you, Miss Willow. As for the cat… well… I cannot wait to see Mrs. Simpson's face when you bring her inside." The butler laughed. "You brighten up this dull place. You always did." George headed through the ornate front door and into the marble-tiled foyer; we followed.

A glistening crystal chandelier glinted above us. Marcus

continued to stare in wide-eyed amazement at the opulence all around him.

"Close your mouth, Tucker. You're drooling." Tate laughed.

"Willow, darling, I'm so glad you're here." My father greeted us in the foyer and air-kissed me on both of my cheeks before pulling me into a strained hug. Physical affection was so difficult for him, and just as awkward for me. Omelet meowed loudly, and I had no doubt in my mind that she was yelling at me for taking her there. Dad looked confused at having a live animal in his home. He certainly must have known that I wasn't going to leave her behind. If he wanted me there, he had to take my cat too.

"I wish I could say I was happy to be here, Dad, but you already know that's not true." I wasn't trying to hurt his feelings, but it was the truth.

"Well, look who's here." Elizabeth's shrill voice echoed through the hall. The sound made me want to stuff a hot poker in my ears. She descended the wide staircase with the regality of a queen. I always felt like she was waiting for me to bow in her presence or kiss her hand. I was more likely to knock her to the ground and rip her hair out than do either of those things.

"Aren't you going to greet your stepmother, Willow?" my father asked, one eyebrow rising in question.

"Of course, it's not like I have any other choice," I responded under my breath. "Hello, Elizabeth. A pure pleasure, as always," I said sarcastically.

"Hmm…." Elizabeth chose to ignore my comment. She noticed Omelet and let out a shriek. "What is that thing? Why is that animal in my house, Barringer? You know I'm allergic to all animals!"

"Well… um… darling, it's not as if Willow could leave her little pet at home," Dad stammered.

"No! I will not have it, Barringer! I positively cannot live in a house where there is an animal. They're dirty, and smelly, and—"

"Fine, that's no problem for me. I'll just go back home." That would be the perfect end to this nightmare.

"You're not going anywhere," Dad said sternly to me before turning to his angry wife. "Darling, the cat will stay in Willow's room. You won't even know she's here."

"If I so much as see one hair from that nasty feline in my home, I will personally—"

"You might want to shut your mouth about my cat, Elizabeth, or I will personally—" Good old Dad cut me off midsentence.

"Ladies, let's remember our manners." My father cleared his throat and gave us both a warning look.

I clamped my mouth shut. I'd really wanted to finish that sentence. Her attack on my cat had crossed the line. Oh well, the time would come for brutal honesty, but apparently today wasn't that day.

Elizabeth tossed her silky blonde hair and turned toward Tate. "Hello, Tate, you're looking well."

"Elizabeth." Tate didn't like her any more than I did.

Finally, she noticed Marcus, who had sort of faded

into the background during our heated family discussion. The surprise on my stepmother's face was hilarious as she greeted him. "Marcus Tucker! What on earth are you doing here?"

Marcus looked more than uncomfortable. He looked positively ill. "I'm Willow's bodyguard. And neighbor. And…." He shrugged, not quite sure what he was to me. I wasn't either, for that matter.

"Unbelievable. Barringer, you could have told me that we would be having three guests," Elizabeth reprimanded my father.

"I did, darling. I said Willow and Tate were coming, as well as her bodyguard." My father sounded irritated.

"Fine, then. I'll go tell Consuela to prepare three rooms in the east wing," Elizabeth huffed.

"I hate to be a bother, but can you please be sure that my room is near Willow's? I know your house is secure, but I need to be close to her at all times," Marcus said.

"Yeah, mine too. I don't trust him to watch her," Tate interjected.

"I cannot believe this. Why are both of you so worried about her? Our home is perfectly safe. What has this world come to?" Elizabeth shook her head, turned on her designer heels, and click-clacked her way across the marble floor and back up the stairs.

My father appeared confused by the entire exchange, and I felt sorry for him. He looked exhausted. I could not imagine what he went through being married to that woman. I knew without a doubt that before Elizabeth went in search of Consuela, her first order of business would be to call her BFF, Cinnamon, and tell her that I was there, with both Marcus and Tate by my side.

I fully expected that Cinnamon would make an appearance the next morning. She wouldn't be able to stay away, and I knew she would be hoping for full disclosure about what was happening between Marcus and me. She had been insane with jealousy when she'd seen us together at Voodoo Doughnut. She also wouldn't be able to pass up a chance to see Tate. His refusal to fall under her spell had always made him that much more enticing.

My father gave Marcus the grand tour while Tate and I headed into the kitchen to say hello to Mrs. Bates, the estate's cook. She was one of my favorite women, and the only person in this house who had shown me any real affection growing up. She squealed and wrapped me into her grandmotherly arms the second I entered the room. That woman had taught me everything I knew about cooking, and I had a soft spot in my heart for her. She reached up and ruffled Tate's blond hair, just as she'd done since he was a little boy. Then she proceeded to make us a "small snack," which in reality was a four-course meal that would put most restaurants to shame.

Nearly thirty minutes later, Dad returned, followed by Marcus, who still looked a bit shell-shocked. My father excused himself, saying that he had work to do, but assured us that Elizabeth would return soon to show us all to our rooms. *I could hardly wait to see her again.*

"Why don't I just sleep in my old room, Dad? Wouldn't

that be simpler? There are empty bedrooms next to it where the guys could stay." I was confused about why the room situation was such a big deal. I'd just assumed I would sleep in the bedroom in which I'd grown up.

"Your bedroom was recently… um… remodeled. Elizabeth has decided to take up painting, and she told me that your old bedroom has the best lighting in the house. She's turned it into an art studio." Dad shifted uncomfortably from foot to foot.

"An art studio? My old bedroom? Of course she has. Because it's not like there aren't thirteen other bedrooms she could have chosen from." The conniving woman knew no bounds.

That room was the last place I remembered spending time with Mom before she died. I didn't have many memories of her, but the few that I did have were tied to that bedroom. We used to play dress up together, and she would lie across my pink ruffled bedspread, underneath the canopy, and read my favorite books. The visions weren't vivid, but those two snippets of time were all that was left in my brain, and taking away my old room was like taking away my mother all over again. My heart squeezed inside my chest, but I pushed the feelings away.

"Willow…." My father tried to think of something to say.

"Don't sweat it, Dad. As usual, my feelings are of no consequence. Besides, it's just a bedroom, right? Didn't you say you had work to do?" I prompted, simply wishing to end the conversation that made me want to weep.

"Er… yes. I'll see you all tomorrow." Dad nodded and quickly excused himself.

Marcus, Tate, and I ate our snacks in silence. I knew both of them were trying to think of something to say to me to soften the blow of finding out my childhood bedroom had been taken over by Elizabeth's latest whim. There really wasn't anything they could say that would make a difference. I knew where I stood on my father's list of importance, and so did everyone else.

A few minutes later, I heard Elizabeth's heels clicking down the hallway and I cringed. She was followed by a small, timid-looking woman, who I guessed was Consuela. I told myself that no matter what she said to me, I wasn't going to react. I wanted nothing more than to get into whatever room they prepared for me and go to sleep.

"This is the maid, Consuela. She will show you to your rooms in the east wing. I'm sure you will all be quite comfortable there. Breakfast is served at nine o'clock sharp. If you want to eat, be sure you're not late. Mrs. Bates is always prompt with our food. If you need anything, ask Consuela. I'll be retiring for the evening." Elizabeth spoke with the air of a royal.

Was I crazy, or was she putting on a fake British accent? I was certain I'd detected one. She'd obviously fallen into the role of mistress of the manor quite nicely. It was all going to her head. Too bad she was a potential murderer.

"Thank you, Elizabeth," I called sarcastically to the back of my retreating stepmother.

As soon as I got the concrete proof that I needed, I would

be all too happy to send her packing. She was going to look fantastic in an orange prison jumpsuit.

"Lead the way, Consuela." I smiled at the shy maid and followed her up the stairs toward the east wing.

She showed each of us to our respective rooms, explained where everything could be found, told us what to do with our dirty laundry, reiterated the time to be downstairs for breakfast, and then quietly scurried away like a little mouse. I felt sorry for the poor woman. I couldn't imagine how stressful it must be to work for Elizabeth.

I was exhausted and couldn't wait to crash into bed. But before I could do that, I had to get rid of my little fan club. "Well, good night, boys. I will see you at the royal breakfast in the morning," I said dramatically.

"I think maybe I should sleep in the room with you. I would feel better if I was close by, in case you need me." Marcus seemed nervous at the idea of leaving me alone.

Watching out for me was a big responsibility for Marcus, especially now that my father was paying him an outlandish sum of money to do so. Enough was enough though. I needed to decompress, and it would be the first time in days that he wasn't glued to my side. I was not going to sacrifice my alone time.

"Well, if you're sleeping in that room, so am I." Tate didn't pull any punches.

"No one is sleeping in that room besides me and Omelet. No offense to either of you, but I need some privacy. Besides, I'm not sure if you noticed or not, but this place is like a fortress. My dad has always been paranoid, and he has a force of his own bodyguards who live in the guesthouse down the hill. I am as safe here as I'm going to get. You both need to get some rest. You can watch me again tomorrow." I smiled at them both before entering the room, closing the door, and locking it behind me.

I collapsed on the plush king-sized bed and breathed a sigh of relief to be alone for the first time in what felt like forever. Omelet jumped on the bed and curled up beside me. As I lay there contemplating the silence, my mind began to churn. I knew the police were still investigating my case, but had not turned up any new leads so far. The fact that they weren't willing to pay for a security detail told me that it wasn't high-priority.

The person I believed to be the prime suspect was mistress of this house. I was on her turf, which made me an easy target. But I also knew that this entire mansion was built with safety in mind, and there were far too many people around for her to do anything to me here. As much as I wanted to be anywhere else, I knew this house was the safest place in the world for me right then—even if the person who wanted me dead was sleeping under the same roof.

Chapter Thirteen

I groaned as a horrific pounding on the bedroom door startled me first thing the next morning. *What could possibly be important enough to wake me from a perfectly sound sleep?* Rolling over in the plush, blanket-clad bed, I covered my head with the pillow and tried my best to ignore the sound.

"Go away!" I yelled in the direction of the door. The unlucky person on the other side was about to get a very large piece of my mind.

But the banging didn't stop. I sighed and reluctantly rolled out of bed and flung the bedroom door open in frustration. Tate, whose hand stopped mid-knock, stared at me in wide-eyed surprise. He swallowed hard and his Adam's apple bobbed up and down in his throat.

"What do you want?" I asked grumpily as I rubbed my tired eyes.

"Um… is that a trick question?" Tate's voice quivered.

"What's that supposed to mean? You're the one who woke me up." I wasn't happy about that at all.

"You… uh… Willow… you're naked," Tate replied quietly.

"What?" By that time, I was fully awake, and I glanced down at myself.

Sure enough, I didn't have a stitch of clothing on my body. Normally, I didn't sleep in the nude. I was always afraid that something would happen in the night, like a fire, and I'd be racing around trying to find something to put on. So needless to say, I was sort of surprised to realize that I had just answered the door in my birthday suit, and I had no idea why.

Then I remembered I'd been so tired last night that I'd stripped down and climbed into bed. I hadn't even bothered to put on my pajamas. From the look on Tate's face, I'd obviously just shaken up his whole morning. I tried to pass it off as no big deal, even though I knew it was. "Oh, yep, looks like I am." I shrugged.

"Well, you need to either put some clothes on, or give me permission to do exactly what I want to do right now, because you are killing me." Tate smiled deviously.

"Nice try. I'll put something on." I stalked over and grabbed my robe, still unhappy about being awakened before I wanted to be. I slipped the silk robe over my body and tied the sash before flopping back on the bed. Tate shut the door behind him and joined me. "Now, why did you wake me up? That was the best night's sleep I've had in days."

"It's eight o'clock. Breakfast is at nine, remember? You need to eat. So I wanted to give you plenty of time to get ready. You hate being rushed in the morning."

"You know me so well. What would I do without you, other than sleep longer?" I laughed and pulled at him until he was lying on the bed next to me. "I'm lucky you're my best friend, even if you do wake me up too early." Having him close to me always made me feel better, even if his protectiveness drove me crazy most of the time.

"I have to go to work today. I hate leaving you here though. I know how your dad makes you feel unwanted, and Elizabeth makes you want to strangle her. Marcus has no idea how to deal with any of that. He doesn't understand that he needs to be a buffer between you and them." Tate sighed. "I wouldn't leave you if I didn't have to." He reached over and grabbed my hand.

He was always so worried that something was going to happen to me. Once again, I had turned his life upside down. I'd been doing that since we were kids.

"It's fine. You have responsibilities other than taking care of me, Tate. Besides, I'll be all right. I'll just be hanging out here in the castle all day. I have a zillion phone calls to make to the insurance company. I have to figure out what I need to do to get the Dancing Crêpe up and running again as soon as possible." I squeezed his hand and scooted closer to him.

Somehow, he always made me believe that everything was going to be just fine. I laid my head on his chest and snuggled in a little closer. Tate had been my rock and my stability for as long as I could remember. Since we were kids, he had always been like a father, brother, and best friend all rolled into one.

Lately though, I had to admit that I was looking at him through different eyes. I wasn't sure when the change had taken place, but somewhere along the lines, it had. My feelings for him now were something that I didn't quite understand, and they terrified me.

It had taken me a while to admit it, but I knew that I was definitely attracted to him in a way I'd never been before. I knew that man as well as I knew myself, yet suddenly, parts of him were a huge mystery to me. I had kissed him more than once, and I thought about kissing him far more often than I wanted to mention. I dreamed about doing a whole lot more than just kissing him.

I wanted to let myself go and follow my heart, but I knew I couldn't be trusted to be in a normal relationship. I could not lose Tate, and if I crossed the line and fell in love with him and things didn't work out, losing him was exactly what would happen. I wasn't sure I could take that risk.

I didn't deserve to have a nearly perfect human being like Tate so selflessly devoted to me. I wasn't nearly good enough for him. He was an amazing, caring guy, and he should have a girl who would willingly throw her heart at him, without hesitating for even a second. With all of my baggage, I didn't know if I could ever be that girl, no matter how hard I tried. I had always been skeptical of love, and I didn't know whether or not that would ever change.

Tate had already taken the plunge; he'd been honest with

me about the feelings in his heart. He'd opened himself up for ridicule, told me he was in love with me, and I hadn't really been able to give him a decent response.

To top it all off, I was also attracted to Marcus, but that sure hadn't stopped me from kissing Tate. I just floated around, kissing men, confusing them, and taking advantage of their feelings for me. Did that make me a terrible person? Obviously, it did. The best thing for everyone concerned was for me to just keep my distance from Tate. Or decide to commit fully to him. Both options scared me.

"You know I'll help you however I can with getting your business up and running again." He smoothed his hand over my hair while he caressed my back in a rhythmic, almost hypnotic motion. I began to tingle from head to toe.

"You're too good to me, you know that, right?" I propped myself up on my elbow and looked down at him. His vibrant emerald eyes held mine, and I couldn't look away. There was such raw emotion there that it nearly stole my breath.

"You know why I would do anything for you." He was once again laying his heart at my feet, just waiting for me to stomp on it.

"Why, Tate? Why me? I don't deserve you." My heart was about to beat out of my chest. Something was happening to me, and I couldn't figure out what it was.

"I love you." His voice was husky.

"Tate… I love you too, so much. I'm just not sure…." But for some reason, I didn't finish the sentence. In spite of the fact that I'd nearly convinced myself to keep my distance, I was being drawn toward my best friend by some magnetic force that I could neither understand nor control.

"Don't overthink it. Just feel it. For once in your life, Willow, just trust your feelings. Trust in what we have, in what we've always had." He pulled my face to his and my lips seemed to have a mind of their own. They weren't listening to my warnings at all. My mouth met his and a thousand fireworks exploded inside my body, but that time I didn't pull away.

I crushed Tate's mouth with my own, fueled by a passion that was stronger than anything I'd ever felt before. Was this what it meant to truly let go? If so, it was a dangerous thing. I felt a freedom that I couldn't explain. I wanted to laugh, scream, cry, and jump up and down all at the same time. *What's going on?*

He flipped me over on my back and the robe slid off my shoulders. He kissed the exposed skin lightly, and then trailed his lips into the hollow between my shoulder and neck. I sighed loudly. I knew we were about to cross that invisible line, but I couldn't seem to stop, and I didn't really want to.

Tate loved me, and I knew he would never hurt me. The only person who could mess this up was me. So before any rational, logical thoughts could enter my brain, I placed both of my hands on Tate's face and pulled his lips to mine again, drowning in the sensation of finally allowing myself to admit that my feelings for him were so much more than I'd understood.

"I want you, Tate," I whispered in his ear.

He groaned and loosened the sash on my robe. His hand

slid across my stomach, and I gasped.

"Are you sure?" He brushed his fingertips lightly across my collarbone.

"I've never been more certain of anything in my life. But I'm begging you, please don't ask me again if I'm sure, or else I might change my mind," I whispered, and then giggled before kissing him again.

I knew what was about to happen, and I wanted it. I was through fighting my feelings. Tate slid his hands across my body, and I breathed in total contentment. This was the instant when I would finally become a normal woman, capable of a mature relationship. This was what letting go and living in a perfect moment felt like.

But then everything came to a crashing halt as we heard a persistent knocking on the bedroom door.

"Just ignore it. They'll go away," I said between kisses, determined not to be interrupted when I'd finally made up my mind.

But whoever it was did not go away. The knocking continued, sufficiently killing the mood.

"Unbelievable." I sighed angrily. I'd finally worked up the nerve to go with my gut, and it was ruined.

"It's okay. There's no rush." Tate covered my mouth with one long, lingering kiss before scooting off the bed to answer the door. I adjusted my robe, retied the sash, and slid under the covers, using the pillows to prop myself up into a sitting position.

"Well, of course it would be you." I heard the tone of Tate's voice as he opened the door, and I knew without a doubt that Marcus was standing on the other side.

"What are you doing in here?" Marcus demanded as he pushed past Tate and entered the room.

"I invited him in. Good morning, Marcus." I smiled.

"Did you sleep well?" He sat down on the side of my bed, and I could read the concern behind his eyes. He was worried about me, and it was more than obvious that he was attracted to me. This situation couldn't possibly be more complicated.

"I slept very well, thank you for asking. Better than I have in days, as a matter of fact. How about you?" It felt awkward sitting so close to Marcus, knowing what had almost just happened with Tate.

"I never sleep well. I always listen to every sound. A couple of times, I heard footsteps in the hall and I went to check on you. It looks like you're just fine though." Marcus glanced back and forth between Tate and me, and at that moment, I knew he could tell that something had changed.

"You should relax. Really. No one is going to hurt me here. My attacker has no idea where I am." I tried to sound convincing, even though I didn't believe my own story. The truth was that I just knew Elizabeth was the one pulling all the strings.

"I'm sure you're right, but unfortunately, relaxing isn't in my nature, especially where you're concerned." Marcus's smile was strained.

I glanced at Tate, who winked at me and grinned. I rolled my eyes at him.

"So, what's on your agenda for the day, Marcus? I have

a lot of phone calls to make to the insurance company, and Tate has to head back into town for work." I tried to steer the conversation in another direction.

"You're my one and only agenda item for the day. Whatever you're doing, that's what I'm doing, until we catch your attacker." Marcus's voice was steely with determination.

Tate cleared his throat from the doorway, and I knew he wasn't happy about the idea of leaving Marcus unattended with me for the whole day. I needed to find a moment alone with him to put his fears to rest before he left. Somewhere in the midst of all of our making out, I'd reached a decision. I was ready to give things between Tate and me a chance.

"Well, it looks like breakfast is our first stop then, Marcus. You heard what Elizabeth said last night. We can't be late, or we starve. I'm going to need to make myself presentable first, and I imagine you'll want to do that too. Why don't you meet me back here in thirty minutes or so?" That would give me plenty of time to talk to Tate.

"Sure, sounds good." Marcus patted my leg, rose from the bed, and headed out the door. "Have fun at work, Tate. I'll take good care of Willow."

I grinned at the infuriated look that crossed Tate's handsome face. He slammed the door shut behind Marcus and put his hands on his hips.

"I don't like this. I can't go to work knowing he's going to have his paws on you all day long."

I scooted out of the bed and walked across the room. I reached out and took Tate's hands in mine. "He's not going to have his paws on me all day long. You have nothing to worry about."

"Of course I do! I know there's something going on between you and Marcus. I'm not blind." Tate's jaw clenched.

"I'm not going to lie. I'm attracted to him, and I know he's attracted to me. But something happened this morning that I didn't expect, Tate." My voice shook with emotion, and I tried not to cry. This could very well be the most important conversation of my life, and I didn't want to get it wrong.

"What are you trying to say, Willow?" Tate looked uncertain.

"I'm trying to say that I do feel something for Marcus," I began.

Tate's phone buzzed and he pulled it out of his pocket. A look of concern came over his face.

"I have to leave early. They're a man short today. Have a good day with Marcus." His voice was tense as he stalked away.

I stood there, mentally punching myself in the face as I watched him walk down the hallway. I had completely messed that up. *Why in the world did I start the conversation with the fact that I felt something for Marcus?* That wasn't at all what I wanted to say. I wanted to tell Tate that I was falling for him. I wanted to say that I was ready to give us a chance. I wanted to say anything other than what I'd actually said.

Like everything else in my life though, I screwed it all up.

Now, he was off to fight fires, and I hadn't told him how I felt. He would spend the rest of the day thinking all sorts of things were going on between Marcus and me. It would drive him crazy.

At that moment, I knew I needed to make it right; I had to. As soon as I figured out how to get him alone, I would tell him exactly how I felt.

Chapter Fourteen

I had just finished dressing and was still trying to figure out what I was going to say to Tate, when I heard a knock on the bedroom door. Marcus smiled as I opened it, and my tummy flip-flopped. The man was undeniably exquisite. His dark hair was still wet, and it was curling playfully around his ears. His chocolate eyes were sweet, dark pools of intensity, and the intoxicating scent of his aftershave wafted into my nostrils. The muscles in his chest and arms rippled through his tight shirt, and my fingertips itched to reach out and touch them.

The entire combination of his full-on yumminess caused me to feel a bit dizzy. He certainly caused a physical reaction in me, but I realized that's all it was. Now I knew for sure where my heart belonged, and I needed to rein it in.

Down, girl, I mentally warned myself.

I couldn't deny the attraction, but I was determined not to act upon it. I wanted to give the thing with Tate a real shot, and in order to do that, I had to keep my distance from Marcus. The fact that he would be glued to my side every day was going to make that difficult, to say the very least. On top of that, I knew he was just as attracted to me. Love and lust were far too complicated, which was why I'd avoided both of them all these years. I must be crazy to contemplate diving into the game.

"You're looking beautiful, as always, Willow." Marcus dazzled me with his thousand-watt smile. "Shall we go to breakfast?"

He extended his hand to me, but rather than take it, I simply patted his arm and answered, "Sure, let's go." He looked a little confused, but smiled and fell into step beside me as we walked through the maze of ornate marble hallways that led downstairs.

When we arrived at the dining room, I noticed that my father was absent, which was really not surprising. He seldom took the time to sit down to a meal, choosing instead to grab his food on the go while he was working. One of these days, all that work was going to catch up with him. I could remember very few family feasts growing up. Most of my life, I ate my meals in the kitchen, surrounded by Mrs. Bates and the rest of the staff. They had been my family.

Elizabeth was seated at the head of the table, ready to preside over us peasants like the queen she believed herself to be. The light from the brilliant crystal chandelier above glinted off her shiny, perfectly straightened hair. I wondered how much time it took her to fix her hair every morning. My idea of fixing my hair was washing it and letting it air dry. I'd never used a hair straightener, but the whole process seemed like a lot of unnecessary work. Personally, I couldn't invest that much time in my own grooming. I had better things to do. I wouldn't be a bit surprised if she had her own hairdresser living somewhere on the estate, just waiting to do her bidding.

To the right of my wicked stepmother, the annoyingly flawless Cinnamon sat twirling her identical hair and talking nonstop, obviously unaware that we'd entered the room. They were like two sickeningly perfect Barbie dolls, and I recalled with a grin how I'd always loved popping the heads off my Barbies.

Cinnamon was dressed in a skimpy little hot-pink number, showing ample tanned leg and cleavage. The tan was obviously fake; after all, this was the Pacific Northwest, and the sun only came out a few times each year. Her outfit was no doubt painstakingly chosen with the knowledge Marcus would be in attendance. It was probably selected for Tate's benefit as well, and I was suddenly glad he wouldn't be joining us. Now that I'd claimed him for my own, at least in my mind, I was feeling quite possessive. If Cinnamon threw herself at him like she'd done all our lives, I knew I wouldn't be able to control the impulse to blacken both of her eyes.

Marcus and I sat to the left of Elizabeth, across the table from Cinnamon, who began to fidget nervously as we took our seats. I couldn't help but notice that she also grew a little pale when she saw her ex-fiancé. So much for the fake tan. I glanced at Marcus, who appeared strangely nervous himself, and I wondered what was happening.

It must be difficult for him to be this close to her after what had transpired between them, and I was sorry he had to experience that. He must really care about my safety to put himself through the turmoil of seeing her again. He was a genuinely good guy, and I wanted him to be happy. Cinnamon better watch her step if she even thought about being nasty to him in my presence.

But in very un-Cinnamon-like fashion, she didn't say a word once we took our seats. She just sat there quietly, barely glancing up from her plate. She pushed her food around in circles and had little interest in what Elizabeth was saying to her. Upon closer observation, I noticed that underneath the veneer of her expertly applied makeup, her eyes were red and puffy, as if she'd been crying. That seemed highly unlikely, given the fact that I was positive the woman had no feelings. And yet, the signs of genuine emotion were all there. It was an interesting turn of events. *Maybe she really is human? Stranger things have happened.*

"Good morning. I trust that the two of you slept well?" Elizabeth interjected her exasperating voice into the silence of the room. I could have sworn that I heard that darned British accent creeping in again. *What is that? She's no more British than I am.* She probably thought it made her sound more refined. It didn't.

"Yes, Marcus and I both slept just fine." I answered for him, as he seemed uncharacteristically mute. *What is wrong with everyone this morning?*

The second I mentioned Marcus's sleep patterns, Cinnamon's head snapped up and she glared at me. "And just how do you know if Marcus slept well or not?"

"Because when I asked him, he told me. Why? What did you think?" I taunted.

I just couldn't help myself. I loved the fact that she was jealous, and I was also pretty pleased that she thought there was something going on between Marcus and me, even if there wasn't.

"Well, obviously that's the only way you would know how Marcus slept. I mean, look at you, and look at him. He has better sense than to mix himself up with some frizzy-haired, freckled hippie whose only selling point is that she was born into money," Cinnamon spewed wickedly, and I felt my face turn red.

One would think that after all the years of her abuse I would be immune to it, but I wasn't. Her hurtful words stung me every time, and I hated that fact. So I did what I always did when I was confronted by a bully—I fought back. It was childish, and probably not my finest moment, but I didn't let that stop me.

"Funny, Cinnamon, considering Marcus's good taste, I wonder how he ever ended up with you," I shot back at her.

"Ladies, please, can we not do this?" Marcus cleared his throat, and his pained expression made me immediately sorry I'd picked a fight with his ex in front of him.

"Sorry, Marcus." I placed my hand on his on top of the table, but the moment our skin made contact, Cinnamon jumped up and ran out of the room in tears, knocking her chair over in the process.

"Well, now look what you've done. You have quite a knack for ruining things, don't you, Willow?" Elizabeth glared at me and threw her cloth napkin onto her plate, which was still full. I didn't really feel bad about ruining her breakfast, because I seriously doubted she would have finished it anyway. "I'll go check on the poor dear." She rose elegantly from her chair and sashayed off after her friend.

"That went well." I sighed. "I really am sorry, Marcus. That wasn't very nice of me. I know that seeing her again can't be easy for you, and I just made it even worse." I apologized profusely, instantly regretting taking the bait from Cinnamon.

"It wasn't only you. She's just as much to blame," he replied sadly.

He was much more upset about seeing his ex-fiancée than I thought he would be. There had to be more to this story, and I had a feeling I knew exactly what was going on.

"Can I ask you something?" I turned toward him and looked right into his eyes.

"Of course, ask me anything," he replied.

"Do you still love her?" I knew the answer before I even asked the question. I think I had known it since we ran into her at Voodoo Doughnut.

"No! Of course I'm not in love with her. That's ridiculous." His eyes darted away from mine and my suspicions were confirmed.

"We're friends, aren't we?" I finally understood that was

exactly all we were.

"Yes, but I thought maybe we were going to be a little more than that," he answered quietly.

"For a while I thought that too. But we know that's just not possible, don't we? Since we both have feelings for other people." I spoke the truth out loud for the first time, and it felt right. "Besides, you told me once that you loved Cinnamon very much and she broke your heart. That doesn't just go away, no matter how much you want it to, even if you are temporarily distracted by someone as wonderful as me." I grinned at him.

"I have to admit, you are a pretty great distraction," Marcus answered. "But what am I supposed to do? You know Cinnamon! She's not the kind of woman I want to be with. She's self-centered, egotistical, materialistic…." He slumped in his chair in frustration.

"I can't believe I'm saying this, but there must have been some… good qualities in her too, right?" I wanted to rip my tongue out of my mouth for even suggesting that Cinnamon had good qualities. I deserved an award for being such a good friend.

"Yeah, she's beautiful, funny, spontaneous, and she was always planning things she knew I would like to do. She made me feel special and wanted." Marcus smiled as his list grew longer.

"That certainly doesn't sound like the Cinnamon I know, so I guess you brought out something in her that no one else could. That has to count for something, right?" I amazed myself for being able to speak kindly about a woman who was my mortal enemy. I was behaving with a maturity that surprised me. Obviously it wouldn't last, so I knew I should hurry the conversation along before the niceness wore off.

"Yeah, but we come from two different worlds. That was always the problem. She's a rich girl. I would probably never have met her if I hadn't pulled her over for running a red light. She runs in circles I couldn't ever hope to join. She has expectations for the kind of life we should have. Her parents have expectations for the sort of husband their daughter should have. I'm a cop, Willow. We're not even close to being in the same league. I can't give her the things she wants." He ran his hands through his hair and sighed.

"But maybe you're the only one who can give her the things she needs. As soon as I saw the two of you, I knew the truth. She loves you, Marcus, and that's saying something, because I didn't think she was capable of loving anyone besides herself. The look she gave you was the first genuine emotion I've ever seen on her face. Maybe things aren't as impossible as they seem." I patted his leg. "You should go talk to her."

"Maybe I will. What about you? I'm assuming that the person who has your heart is Tate, right? I mean, it's obvious to everyone." Marcus chuckled.

"Well, it was obvious to everyone but me until this morning apparently. I haven't even told him how I feel yet." I swallowed hard, still upset about the fact that I had so horrifically blown the conversation with him that morning.

"Tate Randall is crazy about you. That man would walk across burning coals with bare feet if he thought it would get your attention. He's going to be the happiest man on Earth when you tell him. I can't help feeling a little bit jealous. I was hoping that someday you'd feel that way about me."

"I think things are going to work out exactly how they're supposed to for both of us. Cinnamon is a lucky girl, Marcus. And you'll have to forgive me for saying that she doesn't deserve you. And if she breaks your heart again, I will personally rip every blonde hair out of her perfect head."

"I actually believe you would do that." Marcus laughed.

"Oh, I would. I'm crazy like that. Don't ever forget it."

"Your craziness is my favorite thing about you," he replied.

We both turned back to our plates and finished our breakfast in silence, each lost in our own thoughts of how to reconcile our love lives. When we finished, Mrs. Bates came and cleared the table, shooing us away so that she could work in peace.

"I think I'm going to go find Cinnamon. We have a lot to talk about. I still need to keep an eye on you though. Where are you headed?" Marcus asked.

"I have many, many phone calls to make. I'll probably do that from the rec room. You know, I have the perfect idea. You should talk Cinnamon into going for a swim with you. There's a good view of the indoor pool from the rec room, so you could hang out with your girl and keep a watchful eye on me at the same time. Plus, swimming always breaks the ice," I suggested.

"That's a good idea. I'll go find her."

"Okay, I have to run upstairs and grab my phone and paperwork. I'll meet you there."

I started to walk away, but Marcus grabbed my hand. "Thank you, Willow."

"For what?" I asked.

"For being a good friend. And an even better distraction." He grinned.

"Right back at ya," I replied.

Chapter Fifteen

Three hours later, I was contemplating how much force it would take to break the wooden table in front of me with my skull. I wanted to punch someone, throw something, or unleash some other form of aggression. As appealing as it all sounded, I knew it wasn't going to help me with my problems. Nevertheless, I was angry, frustrated, confused, and generally feeling sorry for myself and my predicament.

Never one to enjoy telephone conversations, even on a good day, I was ready to pull my hair out because I was still on the phone talking about what I needed to do to get my food truck up and running again. The insurance payment was being processed, and whenever it arrived it would cover almost everything, but starting over from scratch wasn't going to be cheap. I would still be a bit short on funds, and I'd spent all of my trust fund money in the start-up the first time around.

I had made a modest living, but most of my income went right back into the business, or helped take care of my everyday expenses. I wasn't exactly rolling in the dough, even though my father was one of the richest men in the world. I knew I could ask him for the money I needed, but my pride was strong. I didn't know if I could humble myself enough to admit to him that I might not be able to do everything on my own after all.

I'd made such a big deal about wanting to be completely self-sufficient, but at that moment I was wondering where to go from there. The thought of not being able to start up the Dancing Crêpe again terrified me, but I was determined to figure out a way. No matter what I had to do, I wasn't about to let my dreams slip through my fingers without a fight.

Anger boiled up inside of me when I thought about the fact that someone had burned down my food truck and tried to kill me along with it. Whoever it was seemed intent upon destroying my life, one piece at a time. Whoever wanted me dead had another think coming if they believed I was going to go down easily. They'd picked the wrong girl to mess with. And if that someone was my stepmother, I was bound and determined to find out.

I watched through the window as Marcus and Cinnamon splashed and laughed in the water. It had been interesting to watch it all unfold. They'd made up quickly, and then they'd made out repeatedly. Although I could have lived a lifetime without seeing their public displays of affection, I was happy that Marcus was getting what he wanted, even if it was Cinnamon.

I had to admit, Psycho Barbie seemed like a different person when I watched the two of them together. She wasn't nearly as snide and fake, and she hadn't stopped smiling, really smiling, since they'd had their talk. I had no idea how they were going to compromise and get beyond their obvious differences, but I supposed it wasn't any of my business, unless she hurt my friend; then I would make it my business.

It was hard to believe that someone as wonderful as Marcus could fall for a human being like Cinnamon, but I really hoped she would be good to him. In the short time we'd known each other, Marcus had become my friend and confidant, and although Cinnamon would always be a sore spot between us, I hoped we could somehow get past it.

The more I thought about it, I wondered if maybe Cinnamon were the one who was trying to kill me. She'd never liked me, even if you took Marcus out of the equation. Having me out of her life would probably be a dream come true for her. I wouldn't put anything past her. Maybe she and Elizabeth were in it together.

"Am I interrupting?" I glanced away from the happy couple when I heard my father's voice behind me.

"Nope, just taking a break from the mountain of insurance paperwork I have to climb. Have a seat." I gestured to the chair beside me.

"Um, well, all right, just for a minute though. I have a conference call." He sat down in the chair beside me. "Is your insurance going to come through for you? I hope you had an adequate policy."

"I'm going to be just fine, Dad. Believe it or not, I'm a pretty good businesswoman. I had decent insurance, and the food truck and most of the equipment and supplies will be replaced. The payment is being processed, so I should be back in business before too much longer," I lied.

Having grown up surrounded by money, I had an intense desire to make my own way in life. I felt as if I had something to prove to the world, that I wasn't just another empty-headed girl who was born with a silver spoon in her mouth. I was determined to pursue my own life without the assistance or connections of my wealthy father; unfortunately, it seemed nearly impossible with my current state of affairs. But I wasn't about to let him know that.

"I have no doubt that you're an excellent businesswoman, Willow. You are my daughter, after all. Good business sense runs in our blood. I am… proud… of you. You do know that, right?" It sounded strange to hear a compliment coming from my dad. They had been few and far between in my life.

"Sure, Dad, I guess I know that. Sometimes it's hard to tell though. You've always seemed so disappointed with my life choices," I confessed.

"Several things that you've done have disappointed me greatly, without a doubt. But far more things that you've done have made me exceedingly proud of you. Your mother would be so happy to see the strong, competent woman you've become." In a moment of uncharacteristic sweetness, he reached across the table and grabbed my hand.

"Thank you. I miss her so much." My eyes filled with

tears, and I blinked them away.

"I do too, every day. But I see her very much alive in you. I guess that's why I keep my distance. It still hurts to remember." Dad's admission came as a surprise.

"I know. Thanks for telling me all of this." I smiled at him, feeling as if we'd come to some sort of understanding.

"Enough of this emotional mumbo jumbo." Dad cleared his throat. "I came here to talk about a gift."

"A gift?" I had no idea where the conversation was headed.

"Yes. I think your food truck offers a service to our community, and I want to make sure that it is back in business sooner rather than later. Not to mention the fact that your success looks good for our family. I want to give you a gift." Dad reached into his pocket and pulled out an envelope.

"What are you talking about?" I asked.

"Can't a father give his daughter a gift?" He smirked at me.

"I suppose so," I conceded.

"Inside this envelope is a check for twenty thousand dollars. Now, before you refuse to take it, just hear me out. I know I haven't always been the father you've needed. I don't know how to do that. I'm not good at feelings and emotions. I show my love by giving people things. I know it's not the kind of love you want, but it's all I know how to do. Please, let me help you. Your mother would want it too." Dad's voice grew quiet, and at that moment I knew if I refused I would hurt him deeply.

"You're right. I don't want your money. I never have. However, I will take the gift and I will be grateful, because as much as I hate to admit it, it's exactly what I need right now." I stood up and took the envelope out of his hand, leaned down and kissed his cheek, and smiled.

"It looks like I finally did the right thing at the right time, huh?" Dad grinned.

"You sure did. Don't tell anyone, but you totally saved the day. Thank you," I replied.

"Well, I'm off to make that conference call. Let's just keep this little gift between us. We wouldn't want to ruin either of our reputations." Dad patted me on the back and left the room as abruptly as he'd entered it.

I breathed a sigh of relief, because as much as I always insisted that I could do everything on my own, my father had just completely saved my behind. I needed that money if I was going to make a new start, and somehow he had known that. He'd probably also known that I was too proud to admit it and ask for his help. I sank into the chair again, still in shock that he had managed to come through for me exactly when and how I'd needed him to. Apparently, there was a first time for everything.

Now that I'd averted one crisis, I moved on to the next. I had to find a way to talk to Tate, and the sooner the better. I grabbed my phone and checked to see if I had a new text from him. My heart sank when I saw that I didn't. I'd been stewing about the fact that I hadn't been able to say exactly what I wanted to him that morning.

Tate had it all wrong, and the only person I could blame

was me. I knew I had to talk to him. I had to make things right. Unfortunately, it looked like I wouldn't see him again until tomorrow. That was too long to wait. I needed to see him today, but I had to do it alone.

I couldn't say all the things I wanted to with Marcus the bodyguard glued to my side. No, I needed to come up with a plan, and fast. The icky nervousness in my stomach wasn't going to go away until I told Tate how I felt about him. Making a quick decision, I grabbed the phone and texted him.

Willow: When is your break? I need to talk to you. Something's come up.

I was certain that would get his attention. He might be angry with me, but I knew he was worried about me too. His curiosity would get the best of him and he would want to know what I meant. He wouldn't be able to help himself. Sure enough, almost immediately, my phone buzzed with a follow-up text.

Tate: Should get a break around 8:00 tonight. Call me then.

Willow: Will do. Talk to you later.

What he didn't know was that when eight o'clock that evening rolled around, he wouldn't be getting a phone call from me. Instead, he would be surprised with an in-person visit at the fire station. What I had to say could not be said over the phone. I needed to see Tate's face when I spoke the words. Nothing else would do. The moment was far too important for it to happen via phone, and I wouldn't be able to rest until I told him.

The only problem was my bodyguard, the one that was always there. So the fact remained that I had to come up with a plan to break away from Marcus, and that wasn't going to be easy. Since the attack, I'd done exactly as I was told, with good reason. I knew Marcus was there to keep me alive. I also knew that if I told Marcus I needed to talk to Tate, he would go with me. That would be the logical, rational thing for me to do. I shouldn't risk my safety by ditching Marcus. I should just follow the rules.

However, I'd never been much of a rule follower, and my ability to be logical was wearing thin. When the moment came to actually talk to Tate, I would be a nervous wreck. Did I really want Marcus along for the show? No, I did not. I didn't need any distractions.

Glancing through the window, I saw Marcus and Cinnamon laughing, completely lost in one another and beyond oblivious to everything around them. Cinnamon gave Marcus tunnel vision, and that might work to my advantage. After all, he had barely even looked in my direction for the past three hours.

If I played my cards right, breaking away from him might be easier than I thought. I would simply have to enlist some help, and I knew just the woman. I could use Cinnamon as part of my plan, but she wouldn't do it willingly. I'd have to trick her into it.

A few minutes later, I saw the two of them get out of the pool and dry off. They kissed, Cinnamon whispered something into Marcus's ear, he grinned like the Cheshire cat, and then he headed out the door and into the rec room where I was sitting.

"Looks like everything went well for you." I smiled up at him.

"Yeah, we still have a lot of things to work out, but we both admitted that we still love each other, so that's a start. You probably gathered that by all of the kissing. Sorry about that." He smiled sheepishly.

"Yeah, well, it provided some great entertainment while I talked to the insurance company. It livened up my dull day, so thanks." I rolled my eyes at him.

"I'm going to run upstairs to change. Will you be okay here for a few minutes?" He turned around and continued to stare through the window at Cinnamon while he talked to me.

"Of course, take your time. I'm not going anywhere." *It's going to be even easier than I anticipated.*

Without another word, Marcus headed upstairs. I'd never seen him so distracted. A few seconds later, Cinnamon, who was still parading around in her teeny-weeny orange bikini, entered the room and glared at me.

"Did you enjoy the show? I noticed you couldn't keep your eyes off us. It must be awful to watch the man you want with someone else," Cinnamon said smugly.

"You're the expert on wanting what you don't have, aren't you?" I smiled serenely, knowing I was about to completely throw her for a loop.

"I have exactly what I want now." She dried her long hair with her towel and examined her manicure.

"I wouldn't be too sure of that, Cinnamon. I mean, did

Marcus tell you about what happened between the two of us?" I wasn't going to say anything that wasn't true, but she wasn't going to like it. I knew they would sort it out. It was obvious they loved each other very much. I was simply setting the hook, and I knew she wouldn't resist taking the bait. I was right.

"You're a liar. Nothing happened between you and Marcus. You only wish it had." Although her words denied that what I was saying could be true, I could see the worry behind her blue eyes. She tried her best to conceal it, but she was hopelessly transparent.

"Marcus is an excellent kisser. Those lips and those hands… mmm." I shivered for effect. I knew I'd just pounded the final nail into the coffin.

"Shut up! Marcus loves me. He always has! You're nothing but a job to him." Cinnamon's voice quivered.

"I didn't say anything about love, did I? What we're talking about is pure lust. As a matter of fact, I'm planning to meet Marcus in the boathouse tonight at seven o'clock. If you don't believe me, maybe you should show up and see." The plan was officially set into motion. *Easy as pie.*

"I don't believe you. I trust Marcus." Cinnamon stomped away in a huff.

"Seven o'clock," I yelled at her retreating back.

I congratulated myself for concocting the perfect plan. I was completely confident that at seven o'clock that evening, Cinnamon would be waiting at the boathouse. As soon as I told Marcus that Cinnamon wanted him to meet her there at that time, everything would be in place. They would be distracted by each other, and I would be home free and on my way to declare my feelings for Tate. *It's like stealing candy from a baby.*

Chapter Sixteen

At seven o'clock on the dot, I sat in the back seat of my father's Tesla, breathing a sigh of relief as the car zoomed down the winding driveway and away from Casa Simpson. Jackson, Dad's personal driver, had been more than accommodating when I asked if he could take me into town to get some things from my apartment.

I felt horrible about leaving Omelet alone at Dad's house, but it couldn't be helped. I would be able to make a much cleaner exit alone. I hoped my baby girl would forget about it by the time I got back, although the way she'd yelled at me when I left made me doubt her forgiveness.

Jackson had been our family's driver for years, and I had always been able to convince him to do my bidding. He was a grandfatherly type, and he seemed to have a soft spot for me. Whenever I asked him to take me somewhere, he did it with no questions asked. He was the perfect person to help me carry out my plan.

Right about then, Marcus and Cinnamon would both be arriving at the boathouse. I'd told him earlier I was tired and wanted to take a nap, so he assumed I was in my room. Marcus would innocently be expecting to have some time alone with Cinnamon, and Cinnamon would be expecting to catch Marcus and me in a compromising situation.

I smiled as I imagined the looks on their faces when they realized they'd both been played. I wondered how long it would take them to figure out that I'd set the whole thing up. Marcus would frantically search the mansion for my whereabouts before figuring out that I'd snuck away.

I tried to ignore the nagging guilt I felt, when for the first time, I considered how worried he would be about me. I hadn't even thought about the fact that my father would be furious for letting me get away from him. In a perfect world, that wouldn't happen; and if it did, I would take full responsibility with Dad and smooth it all over once I'd had a chance to talk to Tate. Best-case scenario would be that Marcus and Cinnamon became so wrapped up in each other that they wouldn't even realize I was gone.

My plan wasn't without danger, and even though I knew I was doing what I had to do, a small part of me was afraid of going into the city alone. I understood that it was Marcus's job to watch me for a reason, and I realized the peril was very real. I mean, I had been nearly murdered twice already. The gravity of the situation wasn't lost on me.

Some relationships were too important to screw up

though, and the mess I'd made with Tate had to be fixed. It couldn't wait until tomorrow. As mercurial as my decisions seemed to be, I was afraid I'd chicken out and change my mind if I waited. I'd taken far too much time to figure it all out, but now that I had, I was practically bursting at the seams to let him know. It was probably impulsive, but that's who I was.

The lights of the city shone through the car's tinted windows, and I wiped my sweaty palms on my mermaid-print leggings. I couldn't believe how nervous I was about talking to Tate. I'd never been afraid to talk to my best friend before, but I was keenly aware that he was so much more than that now. I knew he would be happy to hear that I was in love with him, but I still felt apprehensive about actually saying it, knowing that once a thing was said, it could never be unsaid.

Once I took that step, there would be no turning back. Our relationship would be irrevocably changed, and the prospect scared me to death. We would never be *just* best friends again. It was hard to imagine the two of us as anything other than that, but soon—if it all went according to plan—we would be a couple. Everything in my world would be different.

The thought of our lifelong friendship changing made me contemplate flinging open the door of the car and hurling myself into the night, but I refrained. However, I couldn't stop second-guessing myself. *Am I absolutely certain that telling him is the right move?* I mentally urged the car to move faster before I changed my mind and told Jackson to turn around.

The Tesla pulled up in front of my apartment building, and I told Jackson to give me thirty minutes. I suggested that he should drive down the street and grab a bite to eat while he waited for me, and he readily agreed. Apparently, he didn't even think twice about the fact that I might be trying to trick him, or the fact that my life was in danger. He was far too trusting. Anyone else would have insisted on following me inside, which was exactly why I chose him. Before I could rethink my idea, I jumped out of the back seat, waved goodbye to him, and headed inside the building.

A small part of the plan was to run into my apartment and grab some papers I'd forgotten, so telling Jackson that I needed to get some things from my home wasn't a total lie. I actually did need to pick something up. All I had to do was grab the paperwork and then walk three blocks to the fire station to see Tate. Once I was there, I would call Jackson and tell him there was a change of plans and that he should pick me up at the new location. It was basically foolproof. I had carefully thought out each and every detail.

I rode the elevator upstairs to my floor, exited when it lurched to a stop, and walked down the hallway to my apartment. Now that I was there, completely alone, I had to admit that I felt a bit panicky. The last time I'd been in my apartment by myself was the night of the attack. Apparently, I hadn't thought about that particular part of my plan, the part where I entered my apartment without protection.

I realized that I didn't want to go in there at all, and that made me angry. Why should I be afraid to go into my own apartment? I'd lived alone for many years, and I had never been scared until Mr. Hulk busted in and tried to end my life. Since then, I'd been afraid of my own shadow.

"Stop being a baby, Willow. This is your home. Besides, you know that either Cinnamon or Elizabeth is behind all of this, and neither of them has any idea you're here. This is perfectly safe." I gave myself a pep talk as I slid the key into my front door and tentatively went inside.

I flipped on the lights in the foyer, just like always, and glanced around. Everything seemed to be in place. Obviously, I was just shaken up about the whole near-death experience thing, and who could blame me? Even so, I walked briskly into the kitchen, grabbed the paperwork off the counter, shoved it into my purse, flipped off the lights, locked the door, and left as quickly as I'd come.

Hopping on the elevator, I rode it back down to the ground floor. The whole thing had taken less than five minutes. Stepping outside of my apartment building, I breathed a sigh of relief. I was home free now. All I had to do was walk a couple of blocks to the fire station, and Tate would be there. I took a left out of my building and headed in that direction.

What would Tate do when I told him I was in love with him? Would he be surprised? Could he have possibly seen it coming? No, the way I'd left things that morning, he obviously thought I had feelings for Marcus. As a matter of fact, I'd pretty much said that I did. Emotions were a messy business. No wonder I'd royally screwed up that conversation. It didn't matter though. I was about to fix everything.

Continuing to reassure myself, I tried to picture Tate's face. I walked briskly, knowing I needed to get to the fire station in a hurry if I was going to be able to have an actual conversation before Jackson showed up. Maybe I hadn't left myself enough time for everything I needed to say. I stopped walking, grabbed my cell phone out of my purse, and texted Jackson.

Willow: Change of plans. I need a little more time. Pick me up at the intersection just north of the fire station near my apartment at 8:30. Get some dessert whi le you're waiting.

Faster than the speed of light, good old Jackson replied.

Jackson: As long as you're all right, I won't ask any questions. Maybe I'll get some frozen yogurt. See you at 8:30.

I smiled, tossed my phone back into my purse, and continued walking. Jackson was the right man for the job. Everything was going exactly as it was supposed to. I was just around the corner, and my heart was beating wildly in my chest. *This is the moment when your life changes*. Nothing would be the same after that. Waffling again, I wondered if I was making the wrong choice.

As I approached the fire station, I seriously contemplated running back to my apartment and forgetting the whole thing. Maybe telling him was a bad idea. Maybe it was the worst idea I'd ever had. Tate and I had practically been inseparable since first grade, and it had been amazing.

I was the master of messing up good things. It was what I did best. I was probably the most talented life demolisher

I'd ever known. If anyone could take a perfect thing and make a huge disaster out of it, it was me. What if I did the same thing with Tate? What if I took that perfect, caring, compassionate, protective human being and changed him? What if being involved with me turned him into a different person? I knew I could have that effect on people, and more than anything, I was terrified of ruining Tate's innate goodness. *You've gone to a whole lot of trouble to chicken out now, Willow. Snap out of it!*

I thought about earlier that morning, lying next to Tate in bed. I remembered that for just a few minutes, the whole world ceased to be important and the only thing that mattered was the true, perfect love I saw when I looked in his eyes. I remembered the way he had looked at me, as if I were a good, wonderful person, capable and deserving of the love he had to offer. I'd never felt as complete as I did right then, and that's when I knew. I knew that I was in love with him and nothing else mattered. That's what I needed to keep in mind. That's what I was there to tell him.

I looked through the open bay door and saw Tate rolling up a fire hose. A few other firefighters looked like they were restocking the truck with supplies, and yet another was cleaning the fire truck's engine. I heard them laughing and talking while they worked. The fire bay was a hubbub of activity, and I wondered if they had just returned from a call.

I glanced at my phone and saw that it was exactly eight o'clock, which was the time Tate said he would be free. I hoped I wasn't interrupting. Seeing Tate made my heart do a happy little dance in my chest, and I convinced myself that it was time.

Walking slowly through the open door, I cleared my throat, hoping to get Tate's attention. Instead, I got everyone's attention. Every single head in the bay turned my way, and I felt the heat rise in my face, knowing all too well that my cheeks probably matched my hair.

"Can we help you, miss?" An older gentleman, who I assumed was the chief, stopped what he was doing and smiled kindly at me.

"Yes, I'm here to see…," I began.

"She's here for me, Chief Hugo." I heard Tate's voice, and my tummy did a series of flip-flops. *I'm officially standing in the fire station waiting to bare my soul to Tate. This is really happening. There's no turning back now.* The look on his face told me he was more than surprised to see me there.

"Well, Randall, you shouldn't keep the young lady waiting. Don't be too long though," Tate's boss instructed.

"Thank you, sir," I managed to squeak out.

"Let's go out front." Tate grabbed my hand and led me out of the building.

As soon as we were outside, I started babbling. "I'm sorry if I got you into trouble. I probably should have told you I was coming, right?" *It was stupid of me to show up without warning at his job. I'm obviously going about this all wrong.*

"I'm not in trouble, but what are you doing here, Willow? Is everything all right? In all the years I've worked here, you've never just stopped by." Tate's forehead crinkled with worry.

"Yes, everything is fine. I just... um... well...." Suddenly, I had no idea how to say the right words.

"Why are you here alone? Where's Marcus?" Tate looked around in confusion. It was the first time in days that I'd been anywhere by myself, and he didn't fail to recognize it.

"I sort of ditched him. I played a little trick on him. He's probably figured it all out by now, and I'm going to be in big trouble when he finds me." I laughed nervously.

"Ditched him? What trick did you play on him? And what are you doing alone in the city? Never mind. Tell me again why you're here." Tate looked more baffled than ever.

"Well, I'll tell you... there's a good reason why I'm here... a very good reason. I had to see you. I didn't like the way we left things this morning." *There. That's a good start, right?*

"Well, I'll be honest with you, I wasn't too happy to hear that you and Marcus have this mutual attraction, but I suppose, if it's the truth, you shouldn't have to hide it from me." The sadness in Tate's eyes was more than I could bear.

"I'm not attracted to Marcus. I mean, actually I am, but...." *Oh, goodness. This was not going well at all.*

"You don't have to soften the blow. I can take it. We've always been honest with each other. Let's not lose that."

"Okay, just stop talking for a minute. Don't say anything. Please let me wade through the jumble of words that are floating around in my head." I took a deep breath and tried to calm my nerves.

"Sorry. Go on," Tate replied.

"All right, here's the thing. I am attracted to Marcus, and he's attracted to me. But that's not important at all. It's nothing but a physical reaction. It's just crazy hormones. Do you know why that attraction doesn't mean anything? I'll tell you why. Because in spite of that attraction, we both have feelings—genuine feelings—for other people. Marcus is still in love with Cinnamon. I know, right? How could anyone be in love with Cinnamon? But he is! He loves her very much."

My mouth was moving so fast I wasn't sure if I was even making any sense. I stopped talking and took another breath. *Holy smokes, this honesty business is hard!* I knew I was rambling, and probably incoherently, and I realized that I hadn't yet gotten to the most important part. I still hadn't spoken about the crux of the matter. *Hang on to your fire hose, my friend. You're about to get the surprise of your life.* It was now or never.

"The real reason why my attraction to Marcus means nothing is because my feelings for you are so much more than that. Everything else pales in comparison." *There. I've finally said it.*

"What do you mean? What feelings? What are you talking about, Willow?"

Is it me, or does Tate look like he's going to pass out?

"My feelings… the way I… I love you. I know now that I always have, but I didn't understand how much. I had no idea what kind of love it was until this morning. But now I know. I love you." I swallowed hard, knowing there was still more I had to say. "And I'll be the first to admit that I'm crazy and impulsive and a little eccentric. Okay, I'm a lot eccentric." *No reason to downplay my weirdness. He's had a front-row seat to the Willow show his whole life.*

"Tate, here's the deal… you know every awful, embarrassing, incriminating detail about me. I'm not even slightly mysterious to you. But I'm hoping that in spite of all that, you still love me too." I gulped as the words came pouring out finally, straight from my heart. Now all that was left to do was wait for the reaction.

"You love me, babe? Like, for real love? Like the kissing and making out and happily ever after kind of love?" The look on my best friend's face was priceless. He was reacting like he'd just won the lottery. I didn't think the reality of me even came close to that.

"Yeah, like the for real kind of love. But before you start dreaming about rainbows and puppy dogs, I need you to understand that I can't guarantee a happily ever after. I mean, we are talking about me—the girl who is an emotional disaster. But if you're up for it, I can promise you an interesting ever after. Will you take it? Will you take me?" *I don't think I've ever been this nervous before. I feel like I'm going to vomit all over his shoes. That would certainly be memorable.*

"You've always had me. You've had every part of me for as long as I can remember, babe." Tate reached out and brushed the tears off my cheek with his thumb.

Breathing the biggest sigh of relief ever, I stood on my

tiptoes and wrapped my arms around his neck. Excitedly, I pulled his face to mine. Our lips touched, and I knew without a doubt that this was exactly where I was supposed to be. It had only taken me a lifetime to figure it out.

"I so want to take you back to your apartment right now to celebrate. Unfortunately, I have to get back to work. The chief is going to come looking for me, and if he finds me like this, I'll never hear the end of it." Tate cursed under his breath, and I laughed at his frustration. I could definitely relate; a trip to my apartment sounded like heaven right about then.

"There's no rush. We have plenty of time. I just knew I couldn't wait a minute longer to let you know that you had it all wrong about Marcus and me. Now that we're good, I have to take off anyhow. Unfortunately, I have a mess to clean up back at my dad's house. Mr. Bodyguard is going to kill me himself as soon as he sees me, and Omelet hates my guts for leaving her there." I really was going to have a situation on my hands when I got back.

Tate pulled me close and wrapped me in a huge hug. "Wait a minute. You can't be wandering the streets alone. How are you getting back to your dad's? I should ask Chief Hugo if I can drive you."

"No, I've interrupted your work long enough already. Jackson will be here any minute to pick me up," I assured him.

"I'm going to stay right here until he comes," Tate insisted.

"That's not necessary. Go back inside. The fire station

door is open. I'll be safe out here."

"Not a chance. I'm not leaving—" Tate was interrupted by the chief, who poked his head out the door and gently asked whether or not he was planning on coming back to work. Embarrassed, Tate responded, "Yes, sir. I'll be right there." He squeezed me again in a bear hug.

"I have to go. You're sure Jackson is coming? Shouldn't you come and wait inside?" he questioned.

"Jackson won't see me if I'm inside. Don't worry, he'll be here any minute," I replied.

"You know, Marcus is going to be very unhappy with you. I hope it was worth it." His huge smile let me know that it was worth everything I'd had to do to get there.

"It was definitely worth it. So I'll see you back at my dad's house sometime tomorrow?" I couldn't wait to have some real alone time with him.

"Yep, as soon as I can get away, I'll be there."

"Okay, get back to work before the chief comes out here and yells at me." I playfully pushed him back toward the fire station.

"I'll see you tomorrow. You do know you've just made me the happiest man alive, don't you?" Tate flashed a mile-wide grin, and my heart melted just a little bit more.

"We'll see if you still feel that way after being tied down to me for a few months." I laughed, but I was really afraid of messing things up.

"My feelings for you will never change. See you tomorrow." Tate turned and walked toward the building, but right before he went inside he yelled back, "I love you, Willow."

"Love you too, Tate." I felt like I was floating on a cloud. It was ridiculous and sappy, and I didn't care one bit. It was the truth.

I glanced at my phone and saw that it was eight thirty exactly; perfect timing. I also saw that I had five missed calls and ten nasty text messages from Marcus. *It's time to face the music.* I headed up the street toward the intersection where Jackson was supposed to meet me. Tomorrow was going to be perfect, when Tate and I finally had some time alone with everything out in the open between us.

I grinned ridiculously when I thought about how much fun we would have picking up right where we left off that morning. Tate and I made a pretty cute couple, if I did say so myself.

I was off to clean up the catastrophe I'd had to create in order to make this clandestine meeting happen. I was pretty sure that I could smooth it all over. Of all people, Marcus should understand what it felt like to need some time alone with the person I loved. *The person I love....* Those four words were ones I'd never imagined saying. It felt pretty perfect though, and Marcus would have to forgive me. After all, nothing happened. Everything had gone exactly according to plan.

I checked my phone to see if I had a text from Jackson. He should be arriving any second. All of a sudden, I was completely blindsided by a force so strong it nearly knocked me off my feet. A large, heavy object smashed into my head and I felt the darkness closing in all around me. The last thing I heard right before I blacked out was the sound of my phone crashing to the pavement below.

Chapter Seventeen

I woke up in my bedroom, reeling from a headache so intense that I could barely open my eyes. *My head is exploding. I'm sure of it. How did I get back to my apartment?* The last thing I remembered was walking toward the intersection to meet Jackson. I'd been so happy after my conversation with Tate. *Did I dream the whole thing? Is any of this even real? How much time has passed since then?* I had no idea if it was morning or nighttime. Maybe the events of the last several days were all a dream.

I tried to sit up, but lifting my body seemed to take superhuman effort. Rolling over, I winced in pain, and my hands shot up reflexively to grab my throbbing head. *Uh-oh, there's a definite problem.* What was that sticky dampness I felt underneath my hair? I pulled my hand away from my head and held it in front of my eyes. It was covered in fresh blood. *Why is my head bleeding? No wonder it's throbbing.* This was bad; this was very bad.

I removed the pillowcase from my pillow and placed it on the bloody spot at the back of my head, wincing as I realized that applying any kind of pressure was excruciatingly painful. Head wounds tended to bleed a lot, so I tried not to freak out. I knew I had to try to stop the bleeding though. The beginnings of a whopper of a goose egg rose beneath my fingertips. *What's happening to me?* I closed my eyes and tried to remember.

I recalled the conversation with Tate and the surreal feeling that my life was nearly perfect. *Should have known that wouldn't last long.* There had been the whole sappy, floating on air thing, the glancing at my phone, the walking toward the intersection to meet Jackson, and then the forceful blow that had seemingly come out of nowhere.

I remembered the sound my phone made as it crashed to the pavement below me. *Where is it?* I looked around the room, but it was nowhere to be seen. My phone was practically surgically implanted into my palm, so if it wasn't nearby, that was another bad sign. *Think, Willow! How in the world did you end up back at your apartment with a bleeding wound on your head without your phone?*

All at once, the fog in my brain began to clear, and a sick feeling came over me as I realized I knew the answer. This was all some giant cosmic joke. My life as I knew it was about to crash and burn. My hands trembled, but I continued holding the pillowcase to the wound so that I didn't bleed to death while I formulated a plan.

He's back. I understood, without even looking around, that I wasn't alone, and I knew without a doubt he was in my apartment with me. He was out there somewhere, probably waiting for me to wake up so that he could finish me off once and for all. Although, if he wanted me dead, wouldn't he have killed me already? Obviously, I was a much easier target when I was asleep. Thinking of the numerous ways that he'd flubbed up before, I recalled that he wasn't exactly a professional hit man. *Keep your wits about you, Willow. If there is ever a time to be rational and calculated, this is it.*

The first thing on the agenda was hightailing it out of there. I had to make a break for it, and I had to do it fast. He'd already failed at murdering me on two separate occasions, and I was sure he was ready to put an end to our little cat and mouse game.

I contemplated going out the window, but then I remembered that my apartment was several stories up, high in the air. I would certainly plummet to my death if I went out the window. They would be cleaning up bits and pieces of me from the sidewalk for days. The only option was to leave through the front door, but it would be a miracle if I could slip past him undetected.

I'd outsmarted him the first time, and I could probably do it again if I just concentrated. *Do not get distracted.* I needed to stay focused, and most of all, I must avoid engaging with him. I had a nasty habit of talking when I should just shut up, and it was always my downfall.

For the next order of business, if I were going to fight back, I had to have my hands free. Moving quickly, I rolled up the pillowcase and secured it around my head with a nearby cloth headband in an attempt to keep pressure on my wound. I was certain it wasn't the best look for me, but that didn't matter. If I didn't do something to stave off the bleeding, I would probably hemorrhage to death before I had the chance to thwart my own murder.

Glancing down at my body, I was relieved to note that at least I still had on all of my clothes. The fact that I was not naked was one thing I had working in my favor this time around. *Be grateful for small mercies.*

A weapon, I need a weapon. I grabbed the heavy marble sculpture off the dresser beside my bed. I was determined to go into this with at least some sort of bludgeoning device in my hands. If I could get a clear shot of the guy, I'd smash the statue over his head and it would all be over in a matter of seconds. Of course, I understood that was wishful thinking, since nothing ever seemed to go the way I planned. Catching the guy by surprise and cracking his skull open was probably too much to ask for. *A girl can dream though, right?*

The time for action had come. I tiptoed to the bedroom door and glanced out into my living room. *Unbelievable! Now I really am going to smash him over the head with my statue!* To my utter amazement, the mammoth was sprawled out on my couch watching television, completely relaxed, seemingly without a care in the world. He'd certainly made himself comfortable in my home. Of course, this was his second time visiting, so it probably felt quite familiar to him.

Beyond exasperated, I wondered again why he was after me. Who had hired him? It had to be either Elizabeth or Cinnamon! Both women would be overjoyed to have me out of the picture for good. One thing was certain; I was going to get to the bottom of the situation once and for all.

Watching him as he lounged on my couch, eating the popcorn from my pantry, I felt anger take the place of fear. *I am through running from this man!* In what was probably one of my most impulsive moves ever, I tossed aside my plan of quietly sneaking out the front door. Instead, I stomped out of my bedroom, placed myself between him and the television, grabbed the remote, and turned it off. *So much for being rational and calculated, Willow!*

Obviously, I caught him by surprise. He gasped, started choking on a piece of popcorn, and jumped up off the couch with a shocked expression on his face. He continued to cough and sputter, dropping the bowl of popcorn onto my carpet. *Great!* Now I was not only going to have to bludgeon him with the statue, but I'd also have to clean up his snack. He kept choking, and his face turned an alarming shade of purple. *I am not going to do the Heimlich maneuver on that man!* He would just have to snap out of it.

A couple of minutes later, he finally stopped coughing, and I laid into him. "What are you doing in my home again? Why won't you just leave me alone? And what on earth did you hit me in the head with? I have the worst headache of my life!" I yelled at the man while I shook the marble statue in the air.

Truth be told, I probably looked like a lunatic standing

in front of him with a pillowcase wrapped haphazardly around my head while I used a heavy piece of artwork as a makeshift weapon, but I didn't care. Enough was enough. I was going to end the ridiculousness, and I was going to do it immediately.

"I didn't think you'd wake up so soon. I figured I'd at least have time to finish watching *Dumb and Dumber*. I love that movie." He had to be joking, right? *Dumb and Dumber*? It didn't get any more ironic than that. To make matters worse, the idiot looked genuinely surprised to see me standing in my own living room.

"Let me get this straight. I'm lying in bed bleeding to death from a head injury caused by you, and you're sitting on my couch watching my television and eating my popcorn? What sort of hit man are you? Who was stupid enough to hire you?" I was baffled at his obvious lack of mental activity.

"She isn't stupid. She's a smart lady. You take that back." He rose and lumbered toward me, and I realized again just how large he really was. He could literally snap my skinny little body in half with one of his meaty hands, and he could probably manage to do it without even breaking a sweat.

"I certainly won't take it back. She is stupid, whoever she is. And so are you." I knew I should just keep my mouth shut and run away as fast as I could, but keeping my mouth shut had never been one of my strong suits.

"No, you've got it all wrong," he assured me.

As he spoke, his accent became more prominent, although I still had no idea where it was from. He didn't seem to be any more put together this time around. He was just as much the bumbling buffoon as he was the first time. He obviously hadn't been beefing up his hit man skills, and he hadn't even worn his ski mask this time.

He actually looked like a normal, average guy—other than the fact that he was roughly the size of a baby elephant. If I saw him on the street, I realized I wouldn't automatically think *murderer.* It was strange. I found that I wasn't really all that afraid of him. He was clearly inept, and I was pretty sure I could talk him out of hurting me.

"You know, we've met several times now, and I still don't know your name. In my mind, I call you the Hulk, but it would be nice to know who you really are." I was actually very curious about the man.

"I suppose I can tell you my name, since I'm going to kill you anyhow. It's Dimitri." He nodded at me.

"Well, Dimitri, how much money did she pay you? What is the going rate for my life these days? I'm just curious." I decided I had to keep him talking. I needed to get that concrete proof, once and for all, of which woman wanted me dead enough to pay this oaf to take care of it.

"Two thousand dollars, so I better do it right." He laughed at the shocked expression on my face.

"Excuse me, but did you just say two thousand dollars? That's it? That's all I'm worth? I... I'm... completely offended," I stammered. *My life is worth way more than that.* "You really are a dunce to agree to kill a person for two thousand dollars. Which one was it? Elizabeth or Cinnamon? Or maybe both? Who hired you?"

"I don't know what you mean. Who are Elizabeth and Cinnamon?" The intruder looked genuinely confused.

"They are two horribly awful women who want me dead, one probably more than the other. My bet is Elizabeth," I concluded.

"No. I do not work for anyone named Elizabeth or Cinnamon. Apparently someone else wants you dead too. You're a very popular lady." He smirked at me.

"What other woman could hate me enough to hire a hit man? I don't even know that many women, Dimitri. I'm not exactly what you would call a people person," I explained. *That's the understatement of the year.* Another woman wanted me dead; and I had been so certain I had it all figured out. That was an unexpected turn of events.

"Well, I know that my sister wants you dead very much." Apparently, in Dimitri's world, two grand equaled "very much."

"Your sister? Listen, mister, I don't know you, and I certainly don't know any other members of your family. Are you sure you don't have the wrong girl?" This was obviously a case of mistaken identity. I was pretty sure we could clear this whole thing up in about two seconds.

"Oh no, Katya was very specific. Kill Willow Simpson, the crêpe lady. And make sure she's dead this time. That is exactly what she said." He nodded his head to cement his confession.

"Katya? The only Katya I know is…. Wait just a minute…. Do you mean Blinis and Blintzes' Katya? Are you kidding me?" Shocked, I dropped the marble statue, but unfortunately for me it landed right on top of my foot. I squealed in pain and hopped over to the couch where I collapsed and proceeded to howl in agony.

"That looked like it hurt you very much. Would you like an ice pack? I can get you one. I noticed you had a few in your freezer," the hit man offered. I stared at him in amazement when I realized that he was being completely sincere.

An ice pack? He's offering me an ice pack? He's the strangest killer I've ever met. Actually, he was the only killer I'd ever met, but that was beside the point.

"Are you for real? You came here to kill me and you're asking if I want an ice pack?" I tried to ignore the throbbing in my foot. Maybe if I focused on the horrible pain in my head instead I would be able to do it.

"I was raised with manners, yes?" He shrugged his gargantuan shoulders and looked genuinely confused by my reaction.

I'd finally figured out his accent. It was Russian, just like his Russian sister Katya, who apparently hated me enough to want me dead. I'd always known those words she was slinging in my direction weren't complimentary.

"Sure, you have manners. That's why you go around killing people, right? That's a real strange sense of etiquette you have there." I shook my head, which was throbbing so horribly I felt like I was going to vomit. In all honesty though, it didn't hurt as badly as my foot.

My life was one big joke. *Anything that can go wrong will.* If I was going to wrap my brain around what he was saying, I needed to pry some more information from him. "So what you're telling me is that Katya from Blinis and Blintzes is your sister and she hired you to kill me? Why would she do that?"

"Because you are bad for business. Ever since your dancing crêpes moved in, people go to you instead. I'll admit, the Pirouette is delicious, but never tell my sister I said so." His eyes grew wide with fear. Apparently, Katya wore the pants in that family. "That's the problem. You make our business… meh." He pointed both thumbs down to indicate his displeasure.

"So you and your sister are going to kill me over some crêpes?" *He does realize they're just made out of flour, eggs, milk, butter, and a few other simple ingredients, right?*

"Yes, that is the plan. I'm going to kill you. So we should get on with it." Even though he didn't want to do it, his fear of Katya was obviously compelling. My time was quickly running out.

I tried a new approach. "Can't we just talk about this? I'll give you way more than two thousand dollars *not* to kill me."

"It has already been decided. You have got to go. I'm sorry." He shrugged again, looking genuinely apologetic.

"Well, I hope you know I'm not going down without a fight," I warned.

"Yes, you're very feisty. I remember that from the last time," he complimented. "Unfortunately, you're not strong enough to beat me."

With that, he reached out and grabbed me, picked me up

off the couch, and threw me over his shoulder like a sack of potatoes. The whole situation felt a bit like déjà vu. I was pretty sure that was how it all went down before, except the last time I had Marcus to help me. Unfortunately, I'd burned that bridge. *What am I going to do now? Is this how it all ends for me?*

All at once, my front door came crashing open. Marcus barged through it with his guns blazing—and by guns, I meant his fabulous arms. His biceps were practically ripping his shirt at the seams. Like sausages packed too tightly inside their casings, his poor sleeves could barely contain the enormous muscles stuffed inside them. Obviously, I should not have been focused on his arms at that particular moment, but I was only human after all. He looked every ounce the Super Cop that he was.

Tate, my gloriously sexy fireman, ran in behind him, screaming my name like a madman. I took a moment to appreciate the fact that I had my own personal rescue squad, comprised of devastatingly handsome men. A girl could certainly get used to that.

I sucked in my breath as Tate body slammed poor Dimitri, who still had me thrown across his shoulders. In one fell swoop, the giant hit the ground, dropping me on my head in the process. I was certain to have brain damage before the night was over.

I rolled away from the melee and curled into the fetal position with my eyes closed while I listened to the chaos breaking out in my living room. After a couple of minutes, I realized I was still alive, so I thanked my lucky stars and opened my eyes to see what was happening.

Tate was straddling Dimitri, who was struggling like a bucking bronco. My man threw wild punches at the intruder while he proceeded to call him every name in the book. It wasn't long before Dimitri was beaten to a bloody pulp and Tate's knuckles were a mess. *My man's an animal*. He was like some sort of savage beast that had been unleashed from captivity. I was strangely aroused as I watched him. I had never seen him so primal. It was really a sight to behold.

Finally, after Tate had bloodied nearly every part of Dimitri's body, Marcus pulled him away so he could handcuff the perp. It probably wasn't a moment too soon, because I honestly thought Tate was going to kill him. When I heard Marcus reading the Hulk his Miranda rights, I knew I had to interject.

"Excuse me, Marcus, but Dimitri didn't act alone. His sister, Katya, paid him to kill me because of my crêpes. She needs to be arrested too." I wanted to be sure that all responsible parties paid for their crimes.

"That doesn't even make any sense, Willow, but then again, nothing with you ever does." He glared at me, and I knew I was in big trouble. I would have to smooth things over with him at some point.

Marcus turned back to Dimitri and threatened, "If you want to see daylight again, big guy, you'd better give up your sister's location."

The poor man mumbled something incoherently. His face had been virtually destroyed by Tate's fists, and I would probably be finding his teeth in my carpet for weeks. *Poor Dimitri.* Even though he had tried to kill me several times, I felt a little bit sorry for him. He was obviously terrified of Katya, and who could blame him? She was pure evil.

Just then, my father stalked through my broken front door, looking terrified. He was followed closely by Elizabeth and Cinnamon, who of course looked picture-perfect as always. It was a regular old house party.

"What are you all doing here?" I was still trying to figure out exactly how they'd all managed to come to my rescue.

Tate had finally calmed down, caught his breath, and wrapped his hands inside two of my kitchen towels, presumably to stop the bleeding. He grabbed me and held on so tightly I could barely breathe. "I thought I was going to lose you. I cannot lose you, Willow," he said into my ear.

"I'm sorry," I whispered back to him. Turning to everyone else in the room, I continued, "You guys, I'm really sorry. I know I messed up."

"You've got that right," Marcus said loudly.

Tate helped me as I limped to the couch. We both sat down. He noticed my head wound for the first time, and his paramedic training kicked into high gear. He unwrapped the towels from his own hands in order to remove my pillowcase bandage and inspect my wounds. "This is going to need stitches, and your foot looks like it might be broken. We're heading to the hospital. An ambulance is on the way."

"I am not going…." I couldn't finish the sentence due to the pounding ache coursing through my brain. Maybe he was right. I probably should get checked out, because my foot was still throbbing too. I was going to have brain damage and a broken foot. *Great.*

"I'm taking this loser to jail. You and I will have words when I get back. You have a lot of explaining to do. You lied to me. You know, you're lucky you're not dead right now." Marcus shot daggers out of his eyes as he led my attacker toward the front door.

"Marcus, I'm sorry," I called after him. "I know I shouldn't have snuck away from you. It was stupid. But please just believe me when I say that it was for a really good reason."

He stopped and turned back to me before walking into the hallway. "I know it was for a good reason, and since you're still alive, I suppose I'll eventually forgive you."

"You're a good friend. Thanks." I smiled at him as he led my poor hit man away to jail.

My father, Cinnamon, and Elizabeth stood huddled in a corner, looking completely out of place. Suddenly, I heard a meow, and I looked in the direction of Omelet's cat bed in the corner. My head injury must be far worse than I thought; I was hallucinating. Omelet was at Dad's house, right where I'd left her.

But if she was a hallucination, she was a very real one. She jumped off her bed, where she'd been watching the entire scene unfold, and trotted her little cat body across the room. She purred, rubbed against my leg, and then jumped right up into my lap where she happily licked my face.

"I don't understand any of this. Can someone please tell me what's going on? The last thing I remember was getting hit over the head with something. I have no idea how I ended up here, or how any of you knew where to find me. And is my cat real?" I was exhausted, sore, confused, and both my head and foot hurt. I just needed answers to my questions.

Tate pulled me closer to him on the couch, and I gently placed my pounding head on his shoulder. "I'll try to fill in the blanks for you. When you left and I went back to work, I had no idea anything was wrong. About thirty minutes later, Jackson showed up at the fire station. He was in a state of complete panic. Apparently, he arrived at the intersection to pick you up and you weren't there. He assumed you'd come to visit me, since the meeting place was right next to where I worked. Remember that time he gave me a ride to the station when my truck was in the shop last year? The man apparently has great instincts."

Tate shifted his weight, interlaced his fingers with mine, and continued, "When I heard that you hadn't shown up to meet him, I knew something was wrong. We walked toward the intersection, basically retracing your steps, and found your cell phone on the ground, smashed to pieces. I knew you were in danger, so I called Marcus, who by that time had figured out that you'd ditched him to come and see me. He hightailed it over to the fire station, and since neither of us had any idea where you might be, we decided to start at your apartment. When we got here, we heard voices through the door. Luckily, we showed up just in time. It looked like that guy was about to finish you off." Tate took a deep breath and gently kissed me on the forehead.

It was obvious he was holding back a barrage of emotions

for my benefit, and I was glad. If he started getting choked up, I knew I would too, and I didn't want to break down in front of everyone.

"Yeah, you certainly showed up at the right time. I'd pretty much run out of options, and he was determined to kill me, even though he didn't really want to. Apparently, my life's only worth two grand. Who knew? I would have thought a little bit more, wouldn't you?" I attempted a grin, but winced in pain. It felt like my brain was compressed against my skull.

"You are priceless, and I'm going to spend the rest of my life proving that to you." Tate gently tilted my head up and brushed my lips with his. I forgot everything else until I heard my father clear his throat loudly.

"I have no idea what the three of you are doing here." I turned toward Dad, Elizabeth, and Cinnamon, who still hadn't moved from the corner. "And how did Omelet get home?"

"Well, I was upstairs looking for Consuela when I heard the most horrible meowing coming from your room. Your cat was scratching up the door trying to get out. I opened the door and she pounced at me. It was all very strange. I'm telling you, she looked me right in the eyes, almost like she was trying to explain something to me. As you know, I don't like animals. I knew right away that something was wrong, but I thought I was being irrational," Elizabeth explained. "Marcus and Cinnamon realized you set them up right away, but they didn't know why. Marcus thought you were playing a joke on him by making Cinnamon think the two of you would be in the boathouse. They waited for you to wake up from your supposed nap, but after a while, when you didn't surface, they went to your room looking for you. I told them about the strange interaction with your cat, and Marcus's cop instincts were on high alert. His phone rang, and it was Tate, explaining that you'd been abducted, or whatever. Marcus borrowed a car and sped off into the night like a hero. Your father was worried sick about you, and I didn't want him coming here alone, and Cinnamon was worried about Marcus, so we all decided to come and find out what was happening." My stepmother smoothed her hair as she finished her story.

"And did Omelet just call an Uber or something?" I still had no idea how my cat ended up at home.

"Don't be ridiculous, Willow. I wasn't going to just leave her there. Besides, I knew you'd want to see her if… when… we found you. So, I hooked that ridiculous pink leash up to her collar and brought her with me. I'm afraid I couldn't bring myself to maneuver her into that raincoat though." Elizabeth, who almost sounded human, fiddled nervously with the golf-ball-sized diamond around her neck. She looked more suited to be walking the red carpet than stopping a murder, but I supposed that wasn't the point. She'd actually done a nice thing by bringing my cat to me.

"Thanks. That was… very… thoughtful… of you, Elizabeth." I had a hard time speaking the kind words, but I worked through it.

"You're welcome." She nodded politely.

"So I guess you weren't the one trying to kill me

after all, huh?" I blurted, and then swallowed hard. Had I actually said the words out loud? From the shocked looks on everyone's faces, I had.

"You thought I was trying to kill you?" Elizabeth's shrill voice notched up an octave higher. "Are you insane? Never mind, you obviously are."

"Well, I figured it was either you or Cinnamon. You were the two obvious choices after all." I shrugged as the two women gasped in shock at my brutal honesty.

"Willow Simpson! How dare you accuse your stepmother and her best friend of murder?" my father bellowed, and the sound of his voice caused my head to roar with pain.

I placed my head in my hands and mumbled, "I'm sorry, but seriously, you both hate me. It's not so far-fetched."

"We've always had our differences, Willow, but I have never wanted you dead. That would break your father's heart, and believe it or not, I do love him," Elizabeth stated.

For the first time in all the years I'd known her, she sounded sincere. Maybe I'd misjudged her after all. Stranger things have happened.

"I apologize, to both of you." I raised my head and looked at Cinnamon and Elizabeth. "But don't be so uptight. I mean, it's not like the thought has never crossed either of your minds. Be honest. I know that murdering the two of you has crossed mine."

Cinnamon and Elizabeth looked at each other, looked back at me, and burst into laughter. They knew it was true, and I knew it was true. Our relationship would never really change. We would despise one another until the day we died.

It was just a fact of life. For the first time though, I thought Elizabeth's feelings might actually be real as far as my dad was concerned, and that made me happy. Maybe she wasn't completely evil after all.

"Ladies, shall we go?" Dad placed his hand on the small of his wife's back and led her to the front door. Cinnamon followed.

"Thanks for checking on me," I managed before they left.

"Tate, please keep us updated once you get Willow to the hospital. And you'd better take good care of my daughter. I'll be watching you." Dad winked at me before leaving.

About that time, the paramedics arrived on the scene. Tate explained my injuries as he lifted me into his arms and gently placed my body on the gurney. They wheeled me down the hallway, into the elevator, and we all squeezed inside.

When we reached the ground floor, two muscle-bound firemen lifted the rolling bed into the back of the ambulance. Tate jumped inside with me and angled himself so that his face was next to mine.

"That was cutting things way too close, Willow. I almost lost you tonight." He took my hand in his and gently kissed it.

"I'm like a cat. I'm pretty sure I have nine lives." I smiled up at him.

"Well, however many lives you have, I'm glad you'll be spending them with me."

"I can't promise smooth sailing, Tate. Things don't

usually turn out that way for me," I warned.

"Babe, if I'd wanted smooth sailing, I would have never chosen you." Tate's green eyes shimmered in the dim lighting of the ambulance, and I felt my heart constrict with love for him.

"I suppose that's true. You do know me better than anyone, so it's not like you have no idea what you're getting yourself into." I finally understood that Tate was going into this relationship with his eyes wide open.

As the girl who had a tempestuous relationship with feelings and emotions, I knew I was entering uncharted territory. Maybe I would mess it up and Tate would hate me before it was all said and done, but then again, maybe not. A small, strangely optimistic part of me thought we just might be able to make it work. I couldn't promise him a happily ever after, but an interesting ever after I could definitely provide.

Epilogue

"Thank you all so much for coming tonight. When we started coordinating the Fireman's Ball several months ago, we were working toward a goal of one hundred thousand dollars. Thanks to your generous donations, and the wonderful success of this event, I'm overjoyed to announce that we have far surpassed our original goal. I'm pleased to offer this check in the amount of two hundred and fifty thousand dollars to Chief Hugo." Cinnamon smiled perfectly as she shook the hand of Tate's chief and handed him the large check.

"Thank you, Miss St. James. I am overwhelmed with gratitude. I cannot begin to tell you how far this money will go toward making sure that our firefighters have the safety gear they need. Your generous donations will allow us to continue serving our community to the best of our abilities."

Chief Hugo smiled proudly.

Cinnamon and the chief paused for some photographs, and then exited the stage at the front of the country club ballroom. The DJ started a slow song as he invited the immaculately dressed guests out on to the dance floor.

"I can't believe she actually pulled it off." I smiled as Tate swept me into his arms and began dancing. He knew I was a klutz, but luckily he was a strong dancer, so I just followed his lead. "Even if the whole thing did start as a ploy to get your attention, it was actually a pretty great thing she did."

"Yeah, it was. I know the fire station can certainly use the funds. It's really strange, but I'm starting to believe that Cinnamon might actually have a good side."

I followed Tate's gaze across the room and saw Cinnamon, wrapped up in Marcus's arms, dancing the night away with a look of pure happiness on her lovely face. She was dressed in a red, floor-length gown and honestly looked just like a princess as Marcus twirled her across the floor.

Tate was right; being with Marcus had changed her for the better over the past several months, and everyone could see it. The two of them had somehow worked out their differences, and they were planning the wedding of the century. In a couple of weeks, they would be Mr. and Mrs. Tucker.

Rather than be worried for Marcus, who had become one of my closest friends, I found myself feeling excited for him and his bride-to-be. Although I would never have believed it, I'd come to understand that Cinnamon loved him deeply, and she made him happy. I'd never been more pleased to be proven wrong about someone.

Dad led Elizabeth to the floor, and they began dancing as well. She was looking quite glamorous in her white, scoop-neck, sweep-train evening gown. She perfectly accentuated my father, in his tailored black tuxedo. The two of them together looked like a Hollywood power couple, and I smiled. As much as I'd been against their marriage, I had to admit they seemed to be making it work.

Although Elizabeth and I weren't what anyone would call friends, we'd come to a mutual understanding. I finally realized that, even though she was never my choice for my dad, she was his. Despite her bad qualities—and I hadn't forgotten about those!—I believed she really did love him.

My relationship with Dad had also changed over the past few months. I no longer felt like I was a huge disappointment to him, and in turn, he'd started treating me like a responsible adult. Things weren't perfect between us, but we were trying to bridge the gap. He'd really been working on being a better man, and a few months ago he'd proven it in a big way.

When the time came for me to buy a new food truck and reopen the Dancing Crêpe, I'd mentioned to him how awful I felt that the surrounding Cartlandia business owners had suffered because of Katya's vendetta toward me. He'd taken it upon himself to personally visit each of the food truck owners who were impacted by the fire. I discovered that he gave each owner the money they would need to reopen, since like me, not all of their expenses were covered by insurance. I'd never been more proud to call him my father, and because of his generosity, Cartlandia was back in full swing.

As for Katya and Dimitri, they were serving time in prison, and I personally hoped they wouldn't see the outside world anytime soon. It had taken me a while before I realized I didn't have to be afraid for my life anymore, but between Marcus and Tate, I was getting there.

"Have I told you how beautiful you look tonight?" Tate leaned in and whispered in my ear.

"Only about five hundred times, but feel free to say it again. This is probably the last time for quite a while that I'll spend this much time dolling myself up." I grinned.

I did have to admit that I looked pretty darn good. I'd swept my red curls up into a French twist, and I'd even applied makeup. My emerald-green, lace evening gown was fancier than any dress I'd ever worn, and I'd chosen it because it was the exact color of Tate's eyes. Earlier that day, Dad had given me a pair of pearl drop earrings that had belonged to my mother. I'd thanked him profusely through my tears, and I felt like I had a little piece of her with me that night.

"You took my breath away when I first saw you tonight." Tate smiled.

"Well, you're looking pretty handsome yourself. That tux definitely suits you," I complimented.

"Do you want to get out of here for a few minutes, babe? I need some fresh air," Tate asked suddenly.

"Sure," I replied as he took my hand and led me outside.

The night was a little chilly, but at least it wasn't raining. I shivered, and Tate removed his tux jacket and draped it around my shoulders. The sky was uncharacteristically clear, and the stars sparkled like diamonds. We walked hand in hand along the moonlit path that wrapped around the back side of the Country Club.

"Are you happy?" Tate asked out of the blue.

"Like right this minute?" I asked, not exactly sure what he meant.

"Yeah, right this minute, and in general. Are you happy with me?" he clarified.

"Yes, Tate, I'm very happy with you. You know I had my reservations about moving forward in our relationship, but you were right. I was worried for no reason. We seem to be making it work." I smiled up at him and my heart was so full I thought it might explode.

"That's good. I'm glad that was your answer."

We walked around the bend in the path and I was startled to see Jackson, Dad's driver, standing there with Omelet on her leash. She meowed in greeting, and I couldn't have been more confused to see them.

"Good evening, Miss Willow. Hello, Mr. Tate. I'll be on my way now." Jackson handed Omelet's leash to Tate, tipped his hat to me, and began whistling as he walked away from us.

"Why am I the only one who seems surprised to see Jackson and Omelet standing out here in the middle of nowhere?" I asked Tate.

"Because I knew they would be right here, where I asked

them to be," Tate replied.

"What's going on?" I suddenly felt nervous.

Tate reached out and pulled me into an embrace, kissed me softly, then pulled away and took both of my hands into his. Omelet sat obediently on the ground beside us.

"When I was six years old, I met this little red-haired girl. She had freckles all over her face, and she was as sassy as could be. I'd never met anyone like her before. She didn't give a hoot what anyone thought of her, and she turned my whole world upside down. She stole my heart, and I'm pretty sure I fell in love with her that very day, at just six years old." Tate swallowed hard and continued. "Now, twenty years later, she still owns my heart, and I am even more in love with her."

At that point, Tate dropped to one knee and let go of my hands. He reached over and untied something that was attached to Omelet's collar. When he held out the ring with a perfect, sparkling, oval-shaped diamond that I immediately recognized as the one my father gave to my mother, the tears began to fall.

"That little girl is still so much a part of you, the woman I love, and I can't think of anything I want more than to spend the rest of my life with you. Willow Simpson, will you be my wife?" Tate's green eyes glistened with unshed tears.

"Yes! A thousand times, yes." I was laughing and crying at the same time, and when Tate slid my mother's ring onto my finger, I knew she would have been pleased with my choice.

I pulled him to his feet and kissed his lips, hoping I could somehow convey the depth of the feelings that I couldn't put into words. Tate had been my past, my present, and now he was going to be my future.

"I hope you don't mind that I gave you your mother's ring instead of buying you your own. When I asked your father for permission to marry you, it was his suggestion, and I had a feeling you might want it." Tate kissed the hand that held the diamond.

"It couldn't be more perfect, Tate. I know she would have loved you, and now, even though she's not with us, she'll always be a part of our life together."

"Well, I'm glad that went the way I hoped it would. It would have been horribly awkward if you'd said no. By the way, I also asked Omelet's permission, and she wanted to be part of the moment too."

"It's no wonder I love you so much. Nobody else in the world gets me the way that you do." I laughed, imagining Tate asking Omelet's permission to marry me.

"I do get you. I always have. And you get me. That's why this works so well. And I'm the luckiest guy in the world because I get to marry my best friend." Tate took Omelet's leash in one hand and grabbed my hand with the other as we headed back inside to share our news.

At that moment, my life really was perfect. Disaster might very well strike tomorrow, but Fate had given me an epic moment, and I was going to bask in the glow for as long as it lasted. Tate believed he was the luckiest guy in the world, but I thought he was wrong. I was pretty sure that I was the lucky one.

The End

The Pirouette

Recipe by Karen Westhafer (AKA Aunt Sis)

Meyer Lemon Curd:
¾ Cup of sugar
3 large eggs
6 Tablespoons butter
1 Tablespoon lemon zest
2/3 Cup Meyer lemon juice
Pinch of Salt

1.   Combine all ingredients in a 4 quart saucepan.
2.   Cook, whisking on medium-low heat, 15 minutes to 160 degrees (Fahrenheit) on a candy thermometer. Do not boil.
3.   Press plastic wrap onto surface, refrigerate to chill, up to three days.

Crepes:

1 ½ cups of vanilla almond milk
2 Tablespoons sugar
3 eggs, room temperature
1 cup flour
¼ cup butter, melted
1 teaspoon vanilla
Pinch of salt

1.   In a blender, combine all ingredients. Blend until mixture is smooth and foamy. If possible, et batter sit for 15 minutes at room temperature (or up to overnight in the refrigerator).

2.   Heat a medium, nonstick skillet over medium heat. Add ¼-1/3 cup of batter and swirl batter to completely cover the bottom of skillet. Cook until the bottom of crepe is golden, about 2-3 minutes. Using a rubber spatula (or wooden chopsticks), loosen edges of crepe, and then quickly flip. Cook for one minute more, and then slide out of skillet. Repeat with remaining batter.

Dedication

I would like to acknowledge my fantastic publisher, Hot Tree Publishing, as well as the fabulous editors and beta readers I've worked with on this book. Thank you for the words of encouragement, and for letting me know I could do it, especially when it looked like I couldn't! I would also like to acknowledge all the readers who encouraged me to turn the short story of *Love at First Crepe* into a full-length novel. I hope it lives up to your expectations!

About the Author

Heidi Renee Mason is a passionate romance novelist and crafter of your next happily ever after. She loves listening to the voices in her head (from her characters, of course!) and creating worlds in which her readers can lose themselves for a little while. A native of the Midwest, Heidi now resides in the Pacific Northwest with her husband and three daughters.

Connect with Heidi:

WWW.FACEBOOK.COM/HEIDIRENEEMASON

WWW.HEIDIRENEEMASON.WORDPRESS.COM

Please consider leaving a review on the website of purchase.

If you enjoyed Heidi's story, consider checking out her chick-lit romance *Always Hope*.

About the Publisher

Hot Tree Publishing opened its doors in 2015 with an aspiration to bring quality fiction to the world of readers. With the initial focus on romance and a wide spread of romance sub-genres, we envision opening up t alternative genres in the near future.

Firmly seated in the industry as a leading editing provider to independent authors and small publishing houses, Hot Tree Publishing is the sister company to Hot Tree Editing, founded in 2012. Having established in-house editing and promotions, plus having a well-respected market presence, Hot Tree Publishing endeavors to be a leader in bringing quality stories to the world of readers.

Interested in discovering more amazing reads brought to you by Hot Tree Publishing or perhaps you're interested in submitting a manuscript and joining the HTPubs family? Either way, head over to the website for information:

WWW.HOTTREEPUBLISHING.COM

9 781925 448894